BLACK AS NIGHT

and other nightmares

BILLY WELLS

ISBN: 1456303139
ISBN 13: 9781456303136
LCCN: 2010918041

TABLE OF CONTENTS

iv

THE CLOWN AT MIDNIGHT

My name is Charles Royster. All my friends know I am a horror film fanatic, and they tease me relentlessly about the props I set up in my TV room before I watch a horror flick.

I place two life-size movie monsters on both sides of my 55-inch TV. My favorites are Dracula, Frankenstein, The Mummy, and the Creature from the Black Lagoon. Next, I place a life-size werewolf mannequin dressed in a flannel shirt and jeans in the side chair next to the sofa to watch the movie with me. I light one small candle on the coffee table and turn on the overhead fan at its slowest setting. The draft makes the candle flicker eerily and gives the monsters a more ominous presence.

Larry Igou, a friend at work, had given me a DVD to watch this evening. He recommended it as one of the scariest movies he had ever seen. I asked him to join me, but unfortunately, he had other plans or didn't want to take a chance on cardiac arrest viewing the film at my house.

I got home at about 9 p.m., had a few drinks and dinner, and positioned my props to watch *Terror on Tape*. It was almost 10 p.m. when I slid the DVD into the player and sat down next to the werewolf. I turned off all the lights in the house with my remote. The single candle was the only light.

The werewolf stared at me with his constant wolfish grin.

The feature played for one hour and thirty minutes with scenes from the goriest horror movies of all time. One of the most terrifying scenes was when the madman ripped out the buxom blonde's tongue in *Blood Feast*. For a moment, I thought I might throw up, but the sensation mercifully passed.

Wow! Larry was right. I had never seen a horror movie with this much blood and gore. My nerves were shattered as I sat in the dark with my movie monsters watching blood splattering all over the screen and limbs being hacked off. It was a bloodbath in startling color from start to finish.

When the fright fest was over, I sat there exhausted with goose bumps all over my arms and legs and chills tweaking the hairs on the back of my neck. All my monsters seemed to leer at me in the flickering candlelight.

When the credits stopped rolling, the most haunting melody I'd ever heard assaulted my ears as I began to shudder violently. From the blackness on the screen, these words scrolled up: "You will win tonight's trivia contest if you can name the famous person who said, 'A clown is funny in the circus ring, but what if the same clown appeared at your door at midnight…' Call 888-8888, and if you are the first person with the correct answer, you will be eligible for the thrill of your life." A hideous laugh echoed in the background.

I reached for the phone and punched in the number. An eerie voice said, "What is the answer?"

"Lon Chaney, Sr. He said the greatest horror was "the clown at midnight."

"Correct! You are the winner," an eerie voice said. "I will come to you at midnight and give you a thrill you will remember for the rest of your life."

"What? Is this some kind of joke?" I listened for a response, but the line was dead.

It was inconceivable that anyone would come to my house at midnight for the $2.00 rental fee Larry probably paid. I smiled nervously and turned off the TV. It was 11:25 according to the clock on the wall. I sat surrounded by my monsters and pondered my next move.

Then I redialed the number.

Before I could even speak, the voice said, "It's too late. I'm on my way." The line went dead, and no one answered the second and third time I tried to call it off.

I went to the kitchen and grabbed the largest butcher knife I owned and returned to the living room.

My nerves were raw with anticipation as the minutes ticked away. I regretted making the stupid call, terrified at what might happen at midnight.

I paced the floor as the witching hour neared.

The doorbell rang. I thought of not answering, but my curiosity drove me. Before I could reach the handle, the door squeaked slowly open. This made no sense. I knew I had locked it when I came home from work.

I was experiencing "horror overload" when I began gasping for breath. My whole body was convulsing in utter fear as I looked into the darkness beyond the door.

A tall, pale shape stood in the shadows between the columns on the front porch. The street lamp overhead shone down on a white head and the tip of a red, bulbous nose and portions of a gaudy clown suit. In the shadows, I could see two cruel eyes fixed on me from the recesses of his dark, hollow sockets.

From the long, pointed teeth came a voice that would chill a corpse, "A clown is funny in the circus ring, but how do I look standing at your door at midnight?" He tooted a maddening horn and roared with fiendish laughter.

Suddenly, strobe lights from out of nowhere revealed the hideous eyes and teeth in graphic clarity as the seven-foot clown monster advanced toward me in a pulsing, mind- altering motion. Two rows of pointed teeth spread across his face from ear to ear in a horrifying grin.

As he raised his two grotesque claws to strike, he looked down at me and said, "Are you scared?"

"Scared shitless," I said as I plunged the butcher knife into the center of his chest. The giant clown monster rocked back and then teetered forward, gripping my shoulders to steady himself with what felt like rubber claws. A stream of his warm blood soaked my *Phantom of the Opera* T-shirt.

Urine ran down my leg into my shoe as bright lights illuminated the darkness. Three cameramen and my best friend, Larry, ran into view from the bushes screaming in unison, "You don't have to be scared. We're broadcasting this on live TV."

* * *

FAIR GAME

Ben Leonard loved to kill people.

Tonight's victim was a stranger waiting for a subway car to Times Square at 10 p.m. He had seen the man reading a newspaper right at the edge of the track at the base of the stairway and knew he would be an easy kill. Several other people were standing here and there along the track, but none of them were near his victim's section of the platform.

He was disguised with a black Beatle-length wig and fake Tom Selleck mustache. He wore a lightweight black jacket over his black pants and shirt.

Just as the train was reaching the spot where the man was standing, Ben jumped from behind the shadowy column and gave him a hard push into the oncoming seven-line train. Since he stood in the protection of the stairway, none of the blood splatter soiled his nondescript black clothes. The deed completed, he bounded up the steps to the street as the train came to a screeching, grisly halt. He wished he could have remained a moment or two longer to get a better look at his handiwork, but he was only able to get a glimpse of the man's head exploding when the train struck him.

Ben was shaking from the excitement of the kill as he moved quickly down the mostly deserted street. About ten blocks from the station, he decided to stop at O'Douls Bar & Grill for a drink to celebrate. He found his way to the bar and sat down. The only patrons were a couple fondling each other in the corner and a man wearing a Yankees baseball cap watching the game on the large-screen TV over the bar.

Wiping the counter, the bartender asked in an Irish brogue, "What'll ye have, Laddie?"

Ben smiled and said, "A very dry Grey Goose martini."

The bartender filled a martini glass with some ice cubes and water.

"Which way to the head?" Ben asked discreetly.

The bartender pointed to the rear of the restaurant, and Ben unbuttoned his light coat and strolled off in that direction.

When he returned, a man in a business suit was sitting one stool away from the seat he had taken when he entered. He was drinking what looked like a gin and tonic. Ben's martini with three olives rested on a napkin with a small bowl of mixed nuts next to it.

Ben sat on the stool and took a sip of the martini. Replaying the murder in his mind, he grabbed a handful of nuts and ate them. They tasted good. He watched Rivera wind up and throw a fastball that the announcer said was traveling 94 miles an hour.

"You look like you had a hard day," the man in the suit said, giving Ben a warm smile.

Ben wasn't in the mood for conversation, but replied, "I guess you could say that, but after I have another one of these, I'll feel a lot better."

Ben knew that subdued lighting was the preferred ambiance in all NYC watering holes, but this bar was the darkest one he had ever seen. He wondered how a patron could tell if his steak was rare or well done without a flashlight. At least he was confident his wig and fake mustache would not be detected in this dim light.

"I'm Don Lester from Staten Island," the stranger said in shadow. "I just dropped in for a brew before I catch the subway home. I'm an architect, and I work on Third Avenue. What do you do?"

"If I told you what I do, I'd have to kill you," Ben said solemnly.

Don was taken aback by this remark and sat with a shocked expression on his face. After a pause, Ben chuckled and Don finally smiled. "Wow. You looked so menacing for a moment, I thought you might be an ax murderer."

"I assure you I've never used an ax in my work so far."

The two men laughed and sipped on their drinks. Ben ate a handful of mixed nuts and offered the bowl to Don, who passed. They both watched Derek Jeter sliding into home plate ahead of the throw on the TV.

"I can't believe how bad the stock market has been this month," Don said seeing the market statistics pan across the bottom of the screen.

"The economy sucks," Ben agreed. "God knows when we'll come out of it, if we ever do."

Don mumbled some response, but Ben was suddenly deep in thought, surveying the possibilities. He had never killed two people in one day, but he felt the overpowering urge sweep over him. His pulse quickened.

"Don is fair game," he thought. "Just another speck in the gene pool."

"Damn these nuts are good," Ben said, as he felt for the cell phone bomb in his side pocket. He kept it there for just such an occasion. When he saw Don's overcoat draped around the back of the barstool with the right pocket sticking out slightly, he felt his adrenalin kicking in.

A-Rod dove for a hard grounder, scooped it up, and fired to first for the out, just as Don's cell began to ring. When Don pulled the cell from his inside pocket, Ben saw an empty cellophane bag float to the floor. Don turned away and placed his hand over his right ear, while he listened to the caller.

Ben quickly dropped the cell bomb into Don's exposed overcoat pocket. He was sure no one around the bar had seen him. The two in the corner were still fondling each other, and the rest of the patrons had their eyes glued to the baseball game. The score was 2-2 in the bottom of the ninth. He took another pull of his martini and ate some nuts.

Don stowed his cell in his coat pocket and scooped up the cellophane bag from the floor. As he quickly put on his overcoat, he said, "The boss wants me to stop being a bar fly and get home."

"It was nice to meet you, Don. Maybe we'll see each other again sometime."

Without responding, Don hurried toward the door and disappeared into the street.

Ben waited a few moments, then took out his cell and punched the preset number of the phone he'd placed in Don's overcoat. He smiled with satisfaction when he heard it ring and a slight tremor tinkled the glasses over the bar.

He gestured to the bartender to give him another drink and more nuts while he waited for the newsflash on the TV.

When the bartender put down the second martini and another bowl of nuts, Ben said, "These nuts are wonderful. Is this a trail mix? It seems to have raisins or dates in with the nuts."

"I'm sorry, Laddie. These are just plain Planters peanuts. We don't serve anything else."

Ben looked at the nuts the bartender had just put on the counter and ate a few.

"These aren't the nuts you served before," Ben said as he picked up the first bowl that was still on the counter. He handed it to the bartender, who pulled out a small flashlight and shined it into the bowl. There in the bottom was a mixture of nuts, raisins, dates, and what looked like a dead spider rolled in a tight wad.

"Where did this bowl come from?" the bartender asked with a worried expression on his face.

Ben thought of the cellophane bag and knew the answer. His face contorted in horror as he upchucked a mouthful of black spider parts and trail mix all over the top of the bar. Ben felt very sick and slumped from the barstool onto the floor and started to convulse uncontrollably.

He heard the newsflash about a bomb that killed three pedestrians on Third Avenue. He hoped Don was one of them.

When Jeter homered in the bottom of the tenth, Ben's heart had already stopped beating.

* * *

MASQUERADE

My name is Fenwick Warner. I am the master of ceremonies for this year's ghoulish festivities of the Madeira Club's Halloween gala. No expense has been spared for tonight's journey into the abyss of unspeakable terror. The exquisite cuisine has been provided by some of Europe's most celebrated chefs. Brad Simmons, a distinguished member of the entertainment committee, hired a travel agent to provide us a castle in Transylvania to hold the party and requested all the bells and whistles he could provide to make this affair as authentic and unforgettable as possible.

At about ten o'clock, the travel agent had provided more than anyone had expected in terms of gourmet delights, spirits, and unmitigated horror. The gala, without question, was the best party that we had ever conceived in our history. We were finishing a fabulous serving of crème brûlée and opening another bottle of blood red wine when I surveyed the guests at my table. The ambiance was perfect. The candles were dim and flickering eerily, and the cadence of the music was spine tingling as I took note of the bevy of horrific heads that encircled my table of twelve. The Devil sat on my right and the fiendish Frankenstein monster to my left. I placed the goblet that stood before me to my lips and let the scarlet liquid run down my throat.

Suddenly, my eyes beheld the menacing sight of a vampire directly across the table from me. Before the toast, I was sure that a werewolf had occupied that seat. His eyes glared at me, and a smile caressed his lips as two fangs protruded past his bottom lip.

Suddenly, there came a knock on the oaken door and another horrific figure entered the room. The light of the full moon washed over the interior through the open door, and a mysterious burst of fog flooded the room. A fiendish voice on the intercom announced it was the witch from beyond the marshes. She cackled loudly as her mole-infested hand swept a goblet from a serving tray to propose another toast. This was one of many monsters that had made a spectacular entrance during the evening. Each was incredibly authentic and awe-inspiring, but of all the monsters that attended the party, the vampire, who sat at the table across from me, was the most frightening.

The evening of mayhem and monsters went on and on until the hour of midnight. Then after a countdown, just as the second hand reached twelve, all arose and a tremendous roar of laughter filled the room. The cloaks dropped, the masks were removed, and all the lights were turned on. Everyone was finally free to reveal their identity, and most were astonished at who had played the role of the famous movie monsters.

Everyone was pouring another glass of wine when a sudden hush fell over the crowd. In all the confusion and merriment, no one had noticed until now that the person who came to the party as a vampire had not unmasked and was standing alone at the far side of the room. His penetrating eyes swept over the crowd as he stood in a menacing stance with blood trickling from both sides of his mouth. A cruel smile curled around his pointed incisors.

My heartbeat began to accelerate as the room fell deathly silent. Every eye was fixed on the vampire.

"Enough is enough, my good man," I said in my role as the master of ceremonies. "Please remove your mask and let us see who you are."

Suddenly, a tremendous gust of wind burst through the open door. The lights began to flicker violently to the point of being extinguished. The cloak of the vampire fell to the floor as his body faded into a cloud of smoke and the wings of a bat materialized in its place. All stood aghast as the ebony form fluttered over the dining room table and departed through the front door that had blown open. The howling wind outside subsided to a whisper, and the lights returned to normal. Someone turned on the large chandelier, which illuminated every corner of the room.

I heard a scream and turned to see Henry McIver pointing to the floor beneath a corner table. It was then that that we all saw the protruding hand of the masquerader disguised as a werewolf. Upon further inspection, with his werewolf mask removed, we saw that Brad Simmons's jugular was adorned with two bite marks that were still dripping blood.

Our annual Halloween party had been crashed by a real vampire, and Brad Simmons was dead under the dining room table.

Suddenly the night was filled with the howling of wolves and the incessant flutter of bat wings that cast disturbing shadows upon the landscape in the moonlight. The crystal chandelier began to flicker as large bats flew into the room through the gaping open door and one by one materialized into a vampire.

Above the bestial cacophony of shrieks and snarls that prevailed outside in the courtyard, the voice of the travel agent that we had hired to arrange our trip to Transylvania came on the loud speaker.

"Ladies and gentlemen, I hope you have enjoyed the festivities so far. Brad Simmons, who indicated that he had always wanted to meet a real vampire, has gotten his wish, as you have seen. In accordance with Brad's strict instructions for authenticity and our guarantee to host a Halloween party to end all Halloween parties, rest assured that before the sun comes up tomorrow morning, each one of you will meet a real vampire. I am confident this will be something you will remember for the rest of your lives."

I discarded my Cuban cigar in a goblet of brandy and dashed into the coatroom to hide among the coats and scarves. I cowered in the shadows and watched as each vampire sought out a companion for the evening.

Moments later, the coats parted suddenly, and a pale corpse-like face appeared from the gloom. His cold bloodshot eyes looked over me as if he were evaluating a choice steak at the market. His lips parted, and I saw the long pronounced incisors and heard the slurp of his red bloody tongue as he extended a pale hand and said, "Would you care to dance?"

* * *

STREET CINDERWINE

It was early evening when Thomas wandered onto the street. The sun had just disappeared in a burst of oranges and reds on the horizon that was breathtaking from his vantage point on the steep hill. When he reached the crossroads, he looked both ways. To the right he could see neon winking and streams of light darting through the many intersections far off in the distance. He could hear the sound of the crowd mingled with the drone of engines and the intermittent wail of horns blowing. Thomas knew the sound of the rat race well, and turning away, he peered into the tranquility that abided to the left.

Leading away from the city was a time passage filled with trees and stars and mist. His eye caught a glimpse of the word "Cinderwine" written on the street sign as he passed with a smile and a song on his lips.

The houses along both sides of the street were dark with black windows that hung in the October leaves.

After a time, the asphalt turned to stone, and the houses and streetlights were swallowed in the mist.

"Free," he shouted aloud. "How wonderful to throw out one's arm and touch no one… to shout and disturb no one…"

The fog lifted as if swallowed by God, and his eyes beheld a meadow touched by moonlight. The scent of honeysuckle whispered on the breeze, as the dark branches seemed to beckon him onward.

After a time, Thomas wondered how far he'd walked as he strained to read his watch. It was hard to estimate, and he wasn't the least bit tired. Tomorrow was Saturday, and he didn't have to worry about the miserable commute to work. He reflected on his life and the plans he had made when he set out on his life's journey. They were as real then as the city he'd left behind a few hours ago and the road that lay ahead.

Suddenly, he heard the sound of footsteps coming from far off. Could it be that someone else was also searching for the peace of mind he was looking for? He kept his pace, wondering what he might say to the other wanderer. Would it be a quaint hello or a moment of silence as they met and passed each other by? He wondered if he would see the stranger's face in the darkness. Would he be greeted with a smile or with the standard scowl he had seen so often in the city?

A face appeared from the mist. A soft, young girl without a smile stood trembling before him. He wanted so much to share her problems and to be her friend, but he didn't know what to say. He stopped, and the stars faded behind the clouds, and the wind seemed to sigh from her lips.

"Will you believe me?"

"What do you want me to believe?" he replied thoughtfully.

"So many things," she whispered, "that no one else will believe."

"My name is Thomas," he offered meekly as he extended his hand in friendship to the stranger.

"Don't try to touch me!" she screamed. "I'm warning you, you'll be sorry if…."

"Don't worry," he assured her, "I only want to help you, if I can. Nothing more."

"I told him I didn't want to see him anymore, but he wouldn't listen! He kept following me! Then one night, he was waiting for me in the park when I was on my way home from work! I tried to run, but he grabbed me and dragged me into the woods!"

"He raped you?"

"Yes..." she answered solemnly after a long hesitation.

She looked up into his eyes as if to say, "Will you believe me, Thomas?"

After pausing for a moment, she continued, "I didn't know what to do. I was so ashamed. I didn't want to tell anyone, and I didn't see Mark anymore after that night. I just wanted to forget all about it, but not long afterward, I found out I was pregnant. When I finally did tell my parents, they didn't believe that Mark had raped me. They slammed the door in my face and said they never wanted to see me again. Two weeks later, their house caught fire, and the firemen couldn't get to them in time to save them, and now, I'll never be able to see them again, and I'll never have another chance to make them believe me."

Thomas listened intently to her sad story and wanted so much to console her as he searched for the words to make her believe that everything would be all right.

"And when the baby died in her sleep, the doctor said it was my fault!" Her lips stiffened as she spoke, and despite the emotion in her voice, her eyes remained remarkably free of tears. She took his hand and leaned against him seductively, planting a wet kiss on his mouth. Once again, she looked up at him with her sad, beautiful eyes and said, "Do you believe me?"

His heartbeat grew faster and a sudden grip of fear fell upon him as he watched her eyes turn cold and her lips part in a sullen grin.

"And several weeks later," she continued, "when Mark was killed by a hit-and-run driver, all of my friends turned against me. They said it was a shame that no one could prove I was driving the car. So you see, no one will ever believe me."

His heart was ready to explode when he turned on his heel to run, but her blade caught him under the right rib cage, and he fell face first onto the stone pavement.

She turned him over and daintily placed the blade directly under his Adam's apple. She giggled for a moment and began to suck her thumb as she spoke to him in the voice of a little girl.

"No one believed I didn't kill Mommy and Daddy. No one believed I didn't kill the little baby. No one believed I didn't kill Mark, and no one will believe I didn't kill you...."

* * *

DINNER FOR TWO

Frederick was head over heels in love. He had been trying for three days to pop the question to Elisha without success. Each time they were together, he had been so nervous he could hardly breathe. He felt as if his tongue weighed five hundred pounds.

He looked at his cell phone in anticipation. Elisha was supposed to call him at 10:00. It was 9:59. His heart was thumping in his chest like a windshield wiper in a driving rain.

The phone exploded with the *2001: A Space Odyssey* ringtone, and he flipped the phone open and answered in a fit of amorous bliss.

"Elisha, I love you. Will you please marry me?" Frederick blurted excitedly, leaving no chance for wimping out this time.

"Oh, yes, Frederick! I will marry you! I've told my mother so much about you already, but she has no idea how serious our relationship has become. I know she will be so excited to finally get to meet you. I will arrange for you to come to dinner tomorrow evening at about seven o'clock to discuss our nuptial plans with Mother."

"That's wonderful, darling! I'd like so much to meet your mother. Good-bye for now, and remember I'll love you even more tomorrow than I do today."

"Good-bye, darling."

The next evening, Frederick picked up Elisha in his Grand Marquis and followed her instructions to her mother's house. After about a half-hour drive, they approached the small cottage that was situated in a densely wooded area about one mile off the main road. Frederick was surprised to see five late-model cars parked along the left side of the driveway.

"Will there be others joining us for dinner? I was hoping we could have an intimate discussion about the wedding."

"I assure you that you will have mother's full attention and no other guests have been invited to dine with us this evening. Mother loves to collect cars, and these are just a few of the recent models. She has an auto graveyard just beyond the trees, which she is extremely proud of."

"Really, how interesting."

Frederick surveyed the house and the grounds and wondered how many acres her mother's property occupied.

"Does your mother live alone out here? It's so isolated from everything."

"Yes, ever since my father passed away she's been living here alone. After so many years, I guess she's accustomed to the seclusion. She's always lived a very private life."

Unseen at the window, Elisha's mother peered from the shadow of the curtains to the driveway below and watched her daughter and the young gentleman approach the entrance in a lover's embrace. Like all the others, this young man was attracted to her daughter like a moth to a flame. She looked at the twenty-four sets of car keys in her trophy case. She was excited to add a brand new Grand Marquis to her collection. A smile broadened on her hideous face, and her eyes widened as her hand tightened on the butcher knife she had concealed beneath her apron.

She heard the rapping on the front door, and her nostrils flared as she descended the stairs. The pang of insatiable hunger filled her loins.

"What was your mother's reaction to tonight's engagement?"

"She said it was a wonderful idea and that she had been looking forward to having you for dinner."

* * *

BLACK AS NIGHT

The Thompsons were a poor family who lived in a dilapidated farmhouse on a gravel road about three miles from Route 11 in the Shenandoah Valley of Virginia. It was a cold Halloween night in 1963, and the family of four had just finished eating dinner.

Norman Thompson looked out his window at the expanse of his property as he pondered the chores he would do tomorrow. Emily, his wife, was sewing a checkered quilt in the living room by the light of one naked hundred-watt bulb. Their teenage sons, Hank and Jeb, were lying exhausted on the front porch after a hard day's work bailing hay.

Jeb struggled to his feet from a hammock and flexed his aching muscles. He extracted a rock from his pocket, and after winding up like a pitcher on a mound, he hurled it as far into the night as he could. Momentarily, the sound of breaking glass shattered the silence of the dark house that stood in the shadows across the gravel road.

"Damn, Jeb, that was a hellacious throw. You're gettin' pretty accurate in your rock throwin'," Hank complimented as he leaned off the side of the porch and spit out a big chaw of tobacco juice.

"That old house gives me the creeps. I wish somebody would come along and bulldoze it."

"What would be the point? The whole parcel Sam Johnson owned is nothing but a pile of rocks. I'll bet that house will fall down before somebody bulldozes it. It's just not worth the bother." Hank scratched his oily black hair and continued. "Do you know what day it is?"

Jeb paused for a moment and then replied, "Hey, I almost forgot after liftin' all those bails of hay. It's Halloween, and I know what you're gonna say before you even say it."

"Last year, on this very night, with a full moon blazin' just like tonight, we heard the sound of that horse. The hoof beats sounded so strange...like thunder," Hank whispered in his spookiest voice.

"I'll never forget how scared I was," Jeb piped in as he peeled a scab from his thumb.

Hank jumped up from his rocker, and like an actor on a Broadway stage, he motioned in the distance and shouted, "And lo and behold, the horse had a rider, both as black as night." And then he continued in his normal voice, "He looked like he was going to a Halloween party, dressed in black from head to toe and wearing a black mask so you couldn't see his face and a black cape blowing in the breeze like some kind of vampire."

"If it weren't for the moon, we'd a never seen him."

"But we still woulda heard that woman screamin' in that sack," Hank remembered.

"Sergeant Wilkes didn't believe a word we said." Jeb sucked on the scab and spit.

"Sergeant Wilkes and his morons! They never did find who murdered those old maids that lived out near Possum Corners."

"Nope, they never did, but I think we mighta seen their killer that night. He certainly was up to no good."

Jeb rolled a cigarette from a tobacco pouch, lit it, and took a long drag. Sticking out his tongue, he blew several smoke rings, which magically spun in circles, one through another, as he recalled that hellish night one year ago. "I can still hear that poor woman screaming. She knew she'd never see the light of day agin."

"I can't believe Wilkes paid us no mind when we spilled our guts on what we saw. Just because we lied about tearing the stop sign down at Columbia Furnace is no reason to think we'd be lyin' about a murder."

Jeb flicked an ash on the porch and said jokingly, "You still say that old house is not haunted?"

"Yep, I never seen anything bumpin' in the night over there so far."

"What about the Johnsons? They disappeared in the dead of night."

"It don't matter if they disappeared; there's no doubt they were murdered. The coroner said that their blood was splattered all over the house. Some maniac like the man on the black horse probably done it. Not ghosts," Hank said as he watched a bat fly across the face of the moon.

"Nobody will ever live in that house agin' after that. The county can't give the place away, and we live right next door."

"Well, Jeb, I'm gonna turn in before you give me the willies and I have to sleep with one eye open all night."

Jeb smiled and pulled out his crusty wallet. "Since you don't believe in ghosts, I'll give you a dollar to go into that old house and stay 'til morning."

"No way," Hank said as he flicked his cigarette onto the road and went for his wallet, "But I'll raise the stakes to three dollars if you think you've got the balls to spend the night over there."

"I don't need money that bad," Jeb conceded.

The two laughed and went to bed, but visions of ghosts and ax murderers lay heavy on their minds.

The night was uncommonly still as the two teens lay there rolling the things they'd seen last year around in their minds. The moon sailed across the sky and disappeared behind a cloud, and the land was swallowed in pitch-black darkness.

Hank couldn't sleep. All he could think of was the masked rider in black with the flowing vampire cape, the blood, and the house next door. He thought he heard Jeb snoring in the next room, but he wasn't sure.

Jeb was tossing and turning and humming "Faith of our Fathers" into the pillow in a low drone. A cool breeze found the crack at the base of the window and blew a musty curtain across the back of his neck. Jeb's hair stood straight up, and a chill ran down his spine like icy fingers.

He sat up and looked about the room and listened for the slightest sound. The moon had reappeared in the sky, and its light shining through the limbs of the trees outside cast eerie phantoms on the bedroom wall. The open closet door gaped at him in the silence.

Several hours passed, and both brothers were restless in their beds. A sound pricked Hank's ear. Hoof beats. He knew right away that no Mennonite carriage would be out at this time of night. It was just one horse coming down the road. It sounded like thunder coming from far off. He looked at his watch—midnight, Halloween.

Jeb whispered in Hank's ear, "It's him," scaring his brother right off his bed.

"What are you doing in my room?"

"Whadda you think? Are we gonna let him get away again?"

"Let's call Sergeant Wilkes!" Hank suggested as a better alternative. "Let him take care of it."

"You know he won't believe us."

Hank paused to weigh the alternatives and whined, "Let's wake up, Pa!"

"You know what Pa said last time."

"The same thing he says every time." Hank rattled off a few Pa-isms in a stern voice impersonating his father: "Mind you own business. Don't catch a bullet that was meant for somebody else. Don't go hunting wolves unless the wolf is hunting you. Let's face it, Pa's not gonna get involved unless the man in black comes knocking on our door, and maybe we shouldn't either."

"If we don't take the bull by the horns, he's gonna get away," Jeb said with a long face.

"Look, birdbrain, I wanna live. I'm too young to die."

Jeb knew his brother well enough to know that Hank was not going to put his life on the line for a total stranger. He didn't want to take any chances either, but he couldn't stand the thought of letting the murderer get away two years in a row. His family could be victims next year. He grabbed his slingshot and some rock pellets from a drawer and reasoned with Hank: "Hey, let's just see what he's gonna do. We don't have to handcuff him or anything. Let's just see where he goes."

Hank reluctantly joined Jeb, and they sneaked out through the back door and crawled behind some shrubs that faced the old Johnson house.

The autumn wind blew through the old tattered curtains that hung in the windows of the battered house. The full moon was still high in the sky as they watched the rider in black dismount his ebony steed. Hank and Jeb's hearts were pounding in their chests, and they were so excited they could barely catch their breaths.

The figure in black crept into the shadows and disappeared behind the dark house. After what seemed like an eternity, he reappeared with a burlap sack in his arms the same as he had last Halloween. The teens heard the sound of a woman screaming emanating from the sack.

"Time for the police," Hank whispered.

"Hey, by the time they get here this pervert will be gone with the wind. Another poor lady murdered."

The rider in black tied the sack on the back of his mighty steed, mounted, and rode off into the night heading away from the state road and deeper into the country. The teenagers mounted their bicycles and followed as close behind the rider as they could without being seen or heard.

"Where can he be going?" Jeb said blankly. "This road is gonna end in about a mile. There's nothin' out here but the old abandoned—"

"Cemetery! Damn, that's where he's headed all right," Hank answered.

With each section of the road, they were ready to give up the chase and make a run for it into the underbrush that they hunted in with their pa for most of their lives. In spite of the unknown that lay ahead in the black night, they continued to follow the masked rider from a distance on the lonely road.

The boys hid their bikes in the bushes a little before they reached the abandoned graveyard. They continued on foot and were careful not to make the slightest sound. The graveyard hadn't been used as a burial ground for many years. Most of the graves had collapsed, and the old stones were leaning. The grass was long and the trees gnarled and leafless. The wind stirred in the trees and crawled up the back of their necks as they lay still near the entrance to the cemetery.

The man in black dismounted, and lifting the sack from across his saddle, pitched it into a grave that had already been dug. The pitiful screams of the helpless female filled their senses with horror.

"He's going to bury her alive. What kind of monster could do such a thing?" Jeb whispered in disbelief.

"I don't want to find out, so stay quiet or I'm out of here."

Hank and Jeb were too terrified to lift their heads to look at the monster piling the suffocating earth on top of his helpless victim. Her futile screams diminished as each shovelful of dirt filled the grave and sealed her doom.

Finally, the deed was done and the screaming ceased entirely when the woman was finally enveloped in the damp, wormy earth. The rider placed the shovel neatly in its place on his saddlebag and swiftly mounted the bellowing, hellish steed. Without the slightest reservation, he rode off into the night from which he had come.

After the hoof beats disappeared entirely, Hank and Jeb ran to the grave in hopes that they could still save the helpless woman from the horrible fate of being buried alive.

Hank found a piece of stump and Jeb a flat rock with which to dig. It seemed like an eternity before they finally reached the burlap. The worms were blanketing the earthen tomb. Their skin crawled with disgust as they untied the sack.

The whimpering sound of the woman within lifted their spirits as they pulled the burlap away from her head and shoulders. The full moon shone down through her golden tresses. Her neck and shoulders looked like ivory in the moonlight. Her sheer nightgown felt like silk to the touch, and the sight of her breasts heaving under the gauzy negligee was the most erotic sight that Hank and Jeb had ever seen.

Hank felt like a hero as he lifted her into his arms and turned the shadow of her face toward the moonlight, saying, "Jeb, I might have just died and gone to heaven."

"Not yet, dearie," the she-beast cackled as she tossed Hank into the grave like a toy soldier. He heard the sound of bones breaking and looked up to see Jeb's headless body, with arms flailing and blood spewing from the cavern that was his neck. Hank tried to scale the slippery wall, but he was again caught in the vise of her icy fingers. He writhed in agony as the monster playfully harvested his left eye with a long fingernail and popped it into her mouth.

Hank remembered that his pa had once told him "Good guys don't always wear white hats" as the world started to spin.

The last thing Hank saw with his good eye was the horror of her face in the moonlight.

* * *

CHRISTMAS EVE

At 3 a.m. on the night before Christmas, Mark and Nancy Jessup were fast asleep after a hard night of decorating. Their children, Cindy and Aidan, were snuggled in their beds in the next bedroom with visions of video games and Barbie dolls dancing in their heads when something struck the house with a thunderous boom.

Cindy shot up off the pillow, rubbed the sandman from her eyes, and said sleepily, "Aidan, Could that be Santa? Do you think his sleigh crashed into the roof?"

"No, silly, Santa never makes a sound when he comes to deliver presents."

"Well, he must have made a boo-boo this time. I hope Santa and his reindeer are not hurt. Do we have any Band-Aids?"

Aidan ignored her and raced from their room into the dark hallway overlooking the living room with Cindy trailing close behind. He tried to turn on the lights, but they didn't work.

Mark and Nancy were already standing at the head of the stairs staring into the darkness below. They all listened, but not a creature was stirring and certainly not a mouse.

"It's only Santa, Dad," Aidan explained.

"Can we see him, Daddy? Please! Just this once!" Cindy screamed excitedly, jumping up and down, looking like she needed to pee really badly.

"Be quiet, both of you," he commanded as he continued to peer into the black living room.

Something fell over and crashed somewhere below.

"That was the Christmas tree!" Aidan shouted. "Santa is sure clumsy tonight."

"Mark, I'll call nine-one-one!" Nancy said and ran into the master bedroom.

"Don't call nine-one-one. Santa may have to leave before we get our presents," Aidan whimpered.

Cindy started to cry.

"That's not Santa down there," Mark said as he ushered the family into the master bedroom.

"If it's not Santa, who could it be?" Aidan pondered.

"Shush!" Mark ordered.

"The phone is dead, Mark," Nancy said with panic in her voice.

"Where's your cell?"

"It's in my purse on the kitchen table. Where is yours?"

"It's charging on the kitchen counter."

"Damn."

"Aidan, bring me your baseball bat," Mark ordered and rummaged through the end table for a flashlight.

Aidan darted off to their bedroom and returned with a Louisville Slugger that was taller than he was.

Mark grabbed the bat and started into the shadows of the hallway. "Stay here," he said firmly.

"Mark! Don't go down there," Nancy screamed. "Let's stay together."

She continued to call for Mark, but there was only silence.

Nancy and the kids stood at the top of the stairs, waiting and listening.

After a few minutes, Mark returned up the stairs quietly and said, "There's someone down there all right. I saw him standing behind the column next to the TV. He's dressed in white from head to toe, and he's very tall. I'm not going to tangle with him unless I have to."

"Could it be Frosty the Snowman?" Cindy chirped and started to dance again excitedly.

Suddenly, heavy footsteps started up the winding staircase. Mark turned on the flashlight, and they all gasped when they saw a snow-white creature with pointed teeth glaring up at them.

"It's the crate beast from *Creepshow*!" Aidan screamed and retreated into the master bedroom.

The others followed close behind and slammed the door behind them.

After Mark and Nancy had pushed all the bedroom furniture against the door, Mark went to the window and wondered if it could be an escape route.

There came a rustling at the bottom of the door. It sounded like a dog smelling for food. With one heavy blow, the door was torn off its hinges, and the bedroom furniture exploded about the room in various piles of destruction.

In the doorway, the hideous snow beast smacked his lips and bared his teeth as his nostrils snuffled the sweet smell of human flesh.

"Daddy? Don't let it get me! Please!" Cindy screamed. The family cowered in the far corner as the beast raised its gnarled claws to strike.

Mark arose from the bed screaming. His T-shirt was drenched with sweat as he threw up his hands to ward off the creature in his nightmare. His heart was pounding in his chest, and he was gasping for breath.

"You're having a bad dream! Wake up! Everything is all right," Nancy said as she turned on the bedside light and felt his forehead to see if he had a temperature.

"Wow! That was the worst dream I ever had. It was so real. Like nothing I have ever experienced." Mark was still shaking as he looked about the room to see if the world was back to normal and the crate beast was only a monster in a dream.

He laid his head back on the pillow, and Nancy turned off the light. They had to get up early for Christmas morning.

A minute passed, and all was still once more. Mark was still restless as he stared at the ceiling, replaying the horrible nightmare in his mind.

At 3 a.m. something really struck the house with a thunderous boom.

* * *

SNAP

Jennifer awoke from a sound sleep in a strange bed with a lover who was not her husband. Gino, her "Italian Stallion" escort, was still asleep and buried in the covers. She cast a roving eye over Gino's muscular torso and peeked under the covers to further inspect his masculinity.

She smiled and rose from the bed in a sheer negligee, grabbed a more substantial nightgown from a chair, and began to put it on. She moved to the balcony sliders a bit groggy from the heavy drinking last evening and playfully touched a few of the empty glasses en route.

She pulled the cord at the balcony, and the drapes parted. An intense ray of sunlight blinded her momentarily. Adjusting to the light, she saw a man with a camera on the balcony across the street snapping pictures of her. She jumped behind the cover of the drapes and pulled her disheveled nightgown about her partially exposed breasts. She found the drawstring and closed the curtains.

"Christ!" she thought. "Here I am a married woman sleeping with a male escort, and some pervert just snapped a picture of me in my birthday suit."

She extracted a fresh set of underwear from a small suitcase on the floor and made her way to the bathroom. After adjusting the water temperature, she climbed into the tub and let the hot spray run over her for almost forty minutes.

Draped in a white towel, she returned to the suite where her lover had been and started getting dressed. Gino was not in bed. She saw that the balcony door was standing open and the curtains were billowing in the wind.

Fully dressed, she went out on the balcony, but to her surprise, Gino was not there. She looked across the street where the man with the camera had been, and he was gone. She did notice several balconies were full of people looking down. She heard a lot of commotion in the street, and whistles and sirens were screaming. She looked down, and there was Gino, spread-eagled on top of a yellow cab with his masculinity hanging out in all its glory. He was not a pretty site with one side of his face crushed in.

She darted inside. The police were arriving, and a large crowd had formed around the yellow cab. Her only thought was to escape before the police found her room.

She grabbed up her things as quickly as she could and, after surveying the corridor, dashed into the hallway. She took the elevator to the basement level where her car was parked. She rifled through her purse, and while searching for her keys, she discovered her wallet was missing. She knew that she had not removed it from her purse in the room, which meant that someone had taken it. Without any further hesitation, she ran to her car and took off up the ramp that led to the street. The parking exit was not on the street where Gino was sprawled. She saw several police officers directing traffic and talking to people on the street in the distance.

As she pulled out, she saw the man with the camera standing on the corner. She turned away as fast as she could when he looked in her direction. The camera was in his hand, but she didn't know if he had snapped another picture of her as she sped off toward the Lincoln Tunnel.

Jennifer remembered the incident at the Water Club the previous evening when four men who looked like they were just coming from a tryout for "Godfather IV" had a confrontation with Gino. Gino couldn't take his eyes off their table all night and was cautious not to be followed when he left the restaurant. It was apparent that they must have been followed to the hotel.

"What have I gotten myself into?" she lamented as she veered around a slow mover and almost ran over a jaywalker on Tenth Avenue.

Jennifer assumed that her husband, Harry, was probably also stuck in traffic on his way home to New Jersey via the Lincoln Tunnel. She chewed her fingernails and drummed the steering wheel as the traffic snarled even more as she approached the mouth of the tunnel.

She had told Harry on Saturday that she was attending a business meeting in Chicago for the entire week. She loved Harry dearly, but their lovemaking was almost nonexistent of late, and she craved a little more excitement in her life. One of her wilder friends had suggested the escort service, and after thinking it over for a few months, she had decided to take the plunge.

She extracted the cell from her purse and called home. No answer.

She dialed Harry's cell. He answered on the first ring.

"Harry! Harry! Are you home?"

"No, I'm stuck in traffic on Route 80."

"Don't go home, whatever you do! Someone stole my purse, and it has my credit cards and my address inside."

"Did you call the police?"

"No. I can't do that. I believe these are dangerous people, and I can't explain now, but we need to meet somewhere and discuss what we are going to do."

"I thought you were in Chicago."

"No, darling. I didn't go after all," Jennifer confessed. "Look, Harry, I am in serious trouble, and I don't know what to do." Jennifer started crying uncontrollably.

"Where are you now?"

"I just went through the Lincoln Tunnel. Let's meet at the Hilton. Go ahead and check in as a…a…Bill Johnson. Pay cash."

The line was silent for a time.

"I know you have questions, but I'll explain when I get there."

"Don't worry, Jen. Whatever it is, we'll work it out."

Another half an hour passed before she reached the Hilton.

Jennifer checked in at the desk and asked for Bill Johnson's room.

"Yes, your husband has already checked into room 512," The desk clerk said and gave her the key to the room as Harry had instructed. "Take the elevator to the fifth floor, turn right. It will be on the right."

Jennifer took the elevator to five and found the room. She took a long breath, swiped the keycard, and entered without knocking.

The suite was much larger than she had expected. There was a wet bar with a high counter where she placed her purse in front of the bathroom. An empty glass of ice was on the countertop, and two little bottles of Bombay Sapphire were next to the glass. She could hear the sound of the shower behind her. The television was on across the room, and the news was just beginning.

"It's show time," she reflected as she tried to prepare the words to explain to Harry what had happened. She surveyed the papers on the bar that faced the TV.

There was a large gray envelop on the top of the bar with photographs partly visible inside. She picked it up and took the photos out and separated them on the desk. Her face drained of color when she saw pictures of Gino and her at the restaurant and the hotel lobby. There were several shots of her standing partially nude at the balcony window and several of her in her car leaving the parking lot. Her wallet was on the top of the bar next to the photos.

Jennifer stood dumbfounded and was trying to connect the pieces of the puzzle, when a picture of her husband filled the TV screen as the news commentator reported, "Harry Fisher, chief executive at the Omar Corporation, went berserk this afternoon and brutally murdered three of his coworkers at his office located at 14 Wall Street."

The shower stopped in the bathroom behind her.

The commentator continued, "Shortly after Fisher's secretary, Miss Ruth Ann Lloyd, and another colleague, Mrs. Karen Verdone, were found dead with their necks broken, Mr. Oswald Bennett, the CEO of Omar, was shot and killed in front of dozens of eyewitnesses when he tried to intervene...."

Jennifer was mesmerized and stood in a state of shock as the videos of Harry's office and his colleagues continued to fill the screen. The bathroom door squeaked as it opened into the room behind her.

Harry placed his hands around Jennifer's neck as the commentator droned on with more details of the office slayings.

Harry's voice resonated in her ear, "Honey, I had a really bad day at the office...."

Snap.

* * *

VICTIM 13

The serial killer watched the young woman as she walked along the deserted Manhattan Street. It was almost midnight, and a low-hanging fog obscured the sidewalk ahead. The dim streetlamps cast spectral fingers of shadow on the ground as the trees lining the walk trembled in the night wind. Despite the eerie solitude of the surroundings, the woman proceeded toward him without any sign of trepidation.

The killer was amazed how brazenly she had entered his kill zone and how nonchalantly she walked toward her destination without regard to the lateness of the hour or the string of murders that he had perpetrated on these very streets over the past twelve months.

She wore a light raincoat, which the killer knew his scalpel would slice through like pea soup. She was dressed sensibly and didn't carry herself like a prostitute, but the killer questioned who else would be walking alone in this part of town at this hour. The only sounds were her footsteps on the sidewalk and the rustling of the wind in the leaves.

In the pocket of his black raincoat, he concealed the razor-sharp blade. It was the perfect instrument for the task, and the same one he had used on his previous victims. He fancied himself as the modern-day domestic version of Jack the Ripper. In fact, the *Manhattan Post* had nicknamed him Jack Junior. He had been a medical student before he switched his major to law and was well versed in the art of surgery, much like the slayer of prostitutes in London in the 1880s.

Jack Junior tightened his grip on the blade as she approached the spot where he lay in hiding. When she passed the alleyway, he leaped from the blackness upon her. He swiped the scalpel across her torso again and again. The blade swept side to side, up and down, and then he crisscrossed her flesh with Zorro-like precision and flair. He assumed that he must have severed the woman's vocal cords with the first swipe of his blade since the woman had not uttered a sound when he struck her, but immediately slumped to the ground in a heap with no attempt to fend off his attack. He could not see her face in the darkness or assess the extent of damage his handiwork had inflicted, but he was sure that thirty or so deep slashes with the scalpel was sufficient to cause massive hemorrhaging and almost instantaneous death.

He dragged her body deeper into the alley to allow him additional time to extract her heart as a souvenir to place with the others in his collection. This was his trademark and undoubtedly why the media exploited his atrocities like no other serial killer that had come before. He pulled a small flashlight from his left pocket to aid him in the extraction of her heart with the same panache of the gifted surgeon he had demonstrated on the other women. This was victim thirteen. He anticipated the headlines in tomorrow's evening addition like a child anticipating new toys on Christmas Day. He also hoped for another grisly photo of the crime scene to add to his collection.

Suddenly, as he reached down to remove the woman's raincoat, he felt two hairy claws poke through his throat and begin to burrow inside. In the glow of the flashlight, he saw the soft features of the young woman's face morphing into something wolfen with deep-yellow eyes and long jagged teeth that seemed to protrude across her jowls from ear to ear like a picket fence. He tried to scream, but his vocal chords were gone. The she-beast's claws ripped through his jugular like soft butter as blood spurted from his neck and began to pool on the sidewalk. His heart stopped as the beast picked him up and inspected him with a ravenous grin.

A stream of saliva ran from her chin as her jaws gaped open and she began to make a meal of Jack Junior. During the feeding, the she-beast's body had fully transformed into something more animal than human, and she inadvertently squashed the small flashlight with her webbed foot, which returned the alley to pitch-blackness.

After devouring a substantial portion of Jack Junior's body, she gave off a high-pitched squeal that sounded like something between the whine of a hyena and the howl of a wolf.

Her mission completed, the she-beast spread her bat wings and effortlessly scaled the wall of the fifty-story building that stood before her. When she emerged from behind the cooling tower of the skyscraper, she disappeared into a cloudbank that was surrounding the top of the granite structure.

The next day, a trail of blood from the street into the alley led a passerby to discover the ravaged remains of the esteemed Manhattan lawyer. Later that afternoon, the authorities found twelve hearts in the refrigerator of his Park Avenue apartment, along with a beautiful scrapbook of news clipping of his previous victims, which proved conclusively that this was the depraved maniac who had sliced and diced the twelve victims over the past year.

High above the city streets on the highest ledge of the fifty-story skyscraper, a stone gargoyle, half bat and half wolf, sat at the corner of the building waiting and watching with a toothy grin.

* * *

CYCLOPS

Jed Norman received a telephone call from Harvey Hawkins in mid-August 1967. Harvey was a former classmate at Strasburg High School who had moved to Pennsylvania after graduating three years before.

When Harvey attended Strasburg, everyone in the small town knew that his folks were extremely poor. He had been missing his right front tooth for most of high school, and for that reason, he never smiled when they took his picture for the yearbook. Before he moved away, he lived on a farm ten miles off the main highway, Route 11, and was notorious for bumming rides whenever he needed to come to town. Jed assumed immediately that this is why Harvey was calling him now since they had never been friends and hadn't seen each other for three years.

Jed and Harvey exchanged a few pleasantries about current events for a few minutes and then Harvey finally got around to the reason for the call.

"Look, I'm visiting with my grandma for a couple of weeks, and I was wondering if you could do me a big favor and let me catch a ride with you to the Woodstock Fair next week. I'd be happy to help you with the gas since you'd be going out of your way. You always treated me well at school, and I don't know anyone else I can turn to."

Jed rolled Harvey's words around in his mind for a few seconds and finally said, "Sure, I can swing by your grandma's place and pick you up. You can forget the gas. I don't mind doing you a favor."

Harvey's voice cracked with emotion as he continued, "You don't know how much this means to me. To be honest, I already called everyone I know, and they all turned me down. You were my last chance."

"That's OK, you can put the ride on your list of things not to worry about. Your grandma still lives in the green house at Columbia Furnace?"

"She sure does."

I'll pick you up at your grandma's on August twenty-ninth at six o'clock."

"I really appreciate it," Harvey beamed, "August twenty-ninth at six o'clock. I'll be there with bells on."

When Jed hung up the phone he was sorry he had been home when Harvey called, but once on the phone, he had not had the heart to tell him no. He felt sorry for him.

Harvey had always looked much older than his years, and even before he moved to Pennsylvania, he was already showing signs of going bald. He remembered that he had been held back a few grades and was probably close to nineteen when he graduated from Strasburg. He was short and stubby and had a gigantic head for the size of his body. He had always been someone only a mother could love and had very few friends. Since none of the girls in their class would even speak to Harvey, he doubted that he had ever had a date.

The dog days of summer sizzled by, and August 29 arrived in a flash. It was Saturday night, and this was the last night of the annual county fair that had been running all week. When Jed drove up to the green house in Columbia Furnace, Harvey looked like a boy with a brand new toy. He was talking a mile a minute when he got in the car. He was dressed in a yellow cowboy shirt that looked like it came direct from the Grand Ole Opry. He donned a wide-brimmed Stetson hat and had a red bandana tied around his neck. His blue jeans looked brand new. The joy of going to the fair had transformed his personality entirely. He was nothing like the introverted soul Jed had known when they attended classes at Strasburg. It was a welcome change.

"Wow!" Harvey shouted straightening his crooked wire-rimmed glasses. "I can't wait to get to the hoochie coochie shows. I've been saving up all year for this one night."

"You know," Jed mused, "I'll bet almost every boy in the Shenandoah Valley had his first feel of a woman in a hoochie coochie show at the Woodstock Fair."

"Jimmy Yost said he was only twelve the first time he got in. The police stood right outside the tent and watched him go in with his hat pulled low over his eyes and holding up his dollar."

"It's unbelievable," Jed said as he accelerated past a slow car and veered back into the far right lane. "I can't believe the girls actually come out completely nude on a stage no more than eight foot square and go from there."

"With a hundred half-loaded farmers screaming like banshees with their elbows on the stage."

Jed and Harvey pulled into the fairgrounds in a cloud of dust and parked as close as they could to the action. The midway was standing room only, and the tents were decorated with huge banners with two-foot-high words that were shocking to the eye like "Macabre," "Bizarre," and "Weird." It was these shows that interested Jed the most. He had a fascination for humans that were deformed or had more arms and legs than they should have. He'd seen a lady with a long black beard last year and a contortionist who folded his body into a small box the year before.

"I'll meet you right here in front of the Ferris wheel at midnight," Harvey said as he ordered a big hot dog with everything on it.

"Don't be late. I'm supposed to meet Timmy Miller at the Blue Stone Inn at one o'clock," Jed shouted over the din of the crowd and also ordered a hot dog.

Harvey turned away from Jed and disappeared into the crowd in the direction of the hoochie coochie shows. Jed finished the hot dog and strode off toward the freak shows.

On the way down the midway, numerous hucksters propositioned Jed. One man wanted to bet him he couldn't knock down a stand of milk bottles with one throw. Another said that he couldn't put an oversized basketball through a tiny hoop. Another carnie wanted to bet him he could guess how much he weighed within two pounds. Jed resisted these temptations and remembered that Skipper Norman had warned him about gambling at the fair. He said that no matter how easy the task looked, the game was rigged so you could not win. Skipper confessed he had learned the hard way. He had even gotten his nose broken when he tried to get his money back.

Jed had one of his best times ever. In addition to seeing three girlie shows, the various rides like the tilt-a-whirl, the roundup, the scrambler, and the octopus added a welcome variety to the freak shows, which were much better than the previous year. He saw a woman with three breasts. He saw a man with no arms and legs that could lift his body off the ground with his tongue. He saw a cow with four ears and a boy with six toes on one foot. It was fascinating, and the night flew by.

After riding the roller coaster three times in a row and eating an enormous amount of fries and hot dogs, Jed was down to his last two dollars. Before him was the only side show he had not seen. There was a huge sign on top of the tent that read, "See it inside! Once in a lifetime! The Cyclops!"

It was five minutes to twelve. Jed knew he was supposed to meet Harvey at the Ferris wheel at midnight. He decided this show was too good to miss. The "Cyclops" was the last show at the end of the fairgrounds, and there was no one waiting in line. Some of the tents across the way had already closed down. The hoochie coochie shows were mostly dark down the midway, and the final stragglers were marching toward the entrance to exit.

When Jed held up his dollar, the ticket taker gave him an odd look, but he decided to let him into the final show. The Coasters were singing "Little Egypt" as he found a seat in the dark interior. When his eyes grew accustomed to the dark, he saw a scarlet curtain draped across a stage that was raised off the ground. He looked around and discovered that he was the only customer. The Coasters ditty stopped, and an organ that must have been behind the curtain started playing a death dirge like something out of the original *Phantom of the Opera*.

Dum, dum, tee dum, dum, tee dum, tee dum, tee dum....

"Wow!" he thought, "This show is really scary, particularly since he was alone." The curtain started to rise, and he saw a man dressed in a flowing black cape floating above the stage about three feet off the floor. The man's back was facing the audience, and Jed was mesmerized.

As the death dirge continued the suspended man started to turn. He could see thin wires attached to the man's arms and legs, which led off in various directions on all sides of the stage. A strobe light began to pulse and then started to intensify as the suspended man's body turned farther toward the front of the stage.

Jed's jaw dropped as he saw the most horrible sight he had ever seen in a freak show. Right in the center of the man's forehead was a large yellow eye with an enormous black pupil. The yellow orb bulged from its socket and glared in his direction. The grotesque eye reminded him of a squid's eye he had once seen in an old horror movie.

The eye seemed to expand and contract like the beating of a heart. It fixed on him with overpowering, unblinking menace as it advanced toward the seat where he was sitting. Jed sat paralyzed with fear as the strobes accelerated across the hideous face and the death dirge built to an ear-splitting crescendo.

Suddenly, two normal eyes blinked open from their customary position on the suspended man's head, and a flesh-colored material that had filled the eye sockets slid from his cheek and fell to the floor. These eyes, rather than threatening, seemed disoriented and confused as they darted to and fro as if searching every corner of the tent for some kind of nightmarish beast who was preparing to leap upon him and tear him apart. Not finding such a beast, the eyes suddenly fixed on Jed, who was sitting right in front of him. These eyes, rather than menacing like the one pulsating on his forehead, were sad and filled with pain as a tear rolled down the Cyclops's cheek.

A sudden sensation of déjà vu swept over Jed as he looked closer at the horrific figure that was suspended before him. He could see the man's face more clearly now, and although it was totally bizarre, it was also uncannily familiar. He had stitches on both sides of his forehead as if Doctor Frankenstein had just completed giving him a new brain. The big yellow eye that bulged from the middle of its forehead was encircled by crude, black stitches that seemed to be dripping tiny droplets of blood.

Jed was still trying to connect the dots in his mind when the Cyclops's lips parted and it started mouthing Jed's name over and over as the two normal eyes seemed to cry out for help. Jed immediately recognized the oversized head and the missing right front tooth that he had seen many times at Strasburg High. It was Harvey, but the words he mouthed were only gibberish since he had only an empty, bloody cavern where his tongue had been.

The music stopped abruptly as the scarlet curtain swooped down, and the interior of the tent was bathed in a flood of blinding lights.

Jed jumped up from his seat and started running for the exit.

Three carnies with lead pipes stood in his path looking him over to see what kind of freak he could be for tomorrow night's show in North Carolina.

* * *

THE SHELL GAME

Herman put on his heavy, woolen overcoat and gloves and prepared himself for his afternoon constitutional. Locking the door behind him, he painfully proceeded down three flights of stairs and continued to the sidewalk that led to Sinclair Park.

As he hobbled past the redbrick ruin that had been his home for the last twenty years, he looked up at the small window of his efficiency apartment and wondered how long it would be before the wrecking ball would find it. The World War I relic across the street had been leveled to make way for condominiums only a month before. He thought of all the little people who would be displaced, very old ones and very young ones, so many with nowhere else to go. He shook his head and decided that he probably wouldn't be around to see it anyway.

As he hurried along, he thought of his lonely life and the barren woman he'd slept beside for thirty years who never learned to know him. The gray clotheslines behind Sherwood House crisscrossed into the leafless trees where his wife had fallen long ago. It had been a day just like today, cold and overcast, with clouds that looked like snow.

He remembered the cemetery and the few friends that had taken the time to pay their last respects. It saddened him to think that most of those who attended would not be in attendance at his funeral since the majority was pushing up daisies themselves.

The hardest part of growing old was watching your own so-called loved ones disappear one by one as the years whispered by.

The north wind began to stir in the trees as he finally reached the park. He looked at his watch and shook his head sadly. The walk had taken three more minutes than yesterday. His heart fluttered, and he stood totally still, waiting. The feeling passed, and he walked on.

His favorite bench had been taken by a wino that had covered himself with newspapers. He passed the middle-aged derelict with little interest, and even less compassion, and proceeded to his second-favorite bench next to the birdbath. He grimaced with pain as he positioned himself for his favorite pastime—the pedestrian parade.

Ten minutes passed. The sidewalks were empty.

Twenty minutes passed. The wino arose, and the newspapers scattered on the ground around the bench. He stretched with a groan and staggered away in the direction of the Salvation Army soup kitchen.

Thirty minutes more passed. The old man kept checking his watch as if he were waiting for a train that was late. A few snowflakes passed on the sidewalk, but no people.

The temperature was falling as the sun began its descent on the horizon. His feet were getting numb from the cold, but he was determined not to be denied. He continued his vigil defiantly.

Thirty minutes later his suffering turned to rage. He arose and cursed the silent walks that waited for him in the snow.

Another precious day had passed without fulfillment. Tears rolled down his cheek from his tired, lonely eyes as he stood in the empty auditorium that was the park. He looked in all directions, but there was no one visiting the park that day.

"Winter," he grumbled, "the worst of all God's creations." Pain pounded in every one of his arthritic joints as he shuffled off into the bitter cold night in the direction of his apartment. The wind whistled through his ears and cut into every pore like a frozen scalpel.

"Oh, but to be young again," he lamented, "to be renewed once more, to be dealt another hand of body and mind." It wouldn't be the same as it was. His failures passed before his eyes like a thousand clowns, each with a gaudy, ludicrous face. He covered his ears, but he couldn't stifle the laughter that haunted every waking hour.

Ahead in the distance, he saw the church where he had worshipped God for forty years. It filled the sky with beams of light that ascended into the clouds like a golden stairway to heaven. He stood there in the wind and the snow as the message of the twenty-third psalm drifted into his thoughts.

"The Lord is my shepherd I shall not want." But he had wanted all his life and had never received.

"He maketh me to lie down in green pastures; he leadeth me beside the still waters." Lies! Peace, tranquility, security, these were feelings he had never known.

"He restoreth my soul." An untruth! His soul had died with his youth and was buried in an unmarked grave with all his broken dreams.

The streetlights faded in the fury of the storm. The great limbs of the trees along the deserted street were swept down upon him. The wind's icy fingers held him fast in its arctic grip as he staggered blindly onward.

His heart fluttered, and fear gripped his mortal soul. "How stupid," he thought, "to doubt God with eternity so near."

He had earned the right to heaven by following God's laws all of his life, and now, on this night, which could very well be his last one on earth, he had blamed God for his failures.

He threw up his hands to the sky and cried out, "Forgive me, God!"

His words were met with a wall of frozen rain that lashed at his face like buckshot.

"Forgive me, God!" he shrieked at the top of his lungs. And the wind swept up behind him and, with all its force, tried to steal his overcoat from his back. Holding on with a death grip and pulling his scarf tighter about his neck, he teetered on shaky legs and leaned in the direction of the church. The howling wind swirled away like a boomerang and came roaring back into his face as he begged for solace. With each plea for salvation, the wind blew harder and harder.

After hobbling along as fast as his aching, exhausted limbs could carry him, he approached the wrought iron fence that stood in front of the tower of God. But as he extended his hand toward the great door of the cathedral, his foot slid on the ice, and he fell with a sickening thud onto the frozen, clinging cement.

"God! Oh, God!" he screamed and tried desperately to regain his footing. His knees buckled, but he grabbed the wrought iron fence and pulled himself upright.

He stood there in the torrent, groping for shelter, shouting for anyone to rescue him from the penetrating cold. He looked to and fro, but the street was empty. His pleas were unanswered. He tried to keep his balance, but again his feet shot out from under him. When he hit the icy sidewalk, his senses shattered on the pavement like glass.

Dazed and dying, the old man lay still on the sidewalk. His strength was gone, and he couldn't move. All he could think to do was to pray.

"God!" he cried. "Please forgive me."

Suddenly, the wind subsided, and a voice answered, "I have come to take you home."

His heart fluttered, and a smile creased his lips as he opened his eyes and beheld the cross shining on the wall of the church before him.

"I am the life," said the voice, and the wind was snuffed out like a candle.

"Behold, I stand at the door and knock…" said the voice, and the snow stopped in the blink of an eye.

"If any man hears my voice and opens the door, I will come into him," said the voice. And a sudden, heavenly stillness fell upon the lonely street.

The pain left his body, and a peaceful feeling engulfed his senses. He arose effortlessly. His savior beckoned to him, and as he took his hand, he said reassuringly, "We must hurry, my son, for your time on earth will soon be over."

His savior's cloak covered his body like a cloud as they disappeared together into the silent night.

One heartbeat later, a stream of light shone down from the heavens upon the very spot where the old man had fallen on the sidewalk.

"Where is he?" said a voice.

"I fear the answer, Gabriel," replied another regretfully.

"Let us hurry! Possibly there is still time since Father has scheduled his release at precisely this time on the clock of life."

The old man and his savior had reached the pearly gates when the two messengers stood frozen in fear in the distance and began to weep.

The old man never saw them as he passed through the hallowed gates. A broad smile beamed on his face as his heart fluttered and began its final beating. He recited the beginning of chapter three of Revelations, "Behold, a door was opened in heaven: and the first voice which I heard was as it were of a trumpet talking to me; which said, come up hither, and I will show thee things which must be hereafter."

And just at that split second, his heart stopped forever; the gate slammed shut on his soul. A mournful bell began to toll as the beautiful songs of the angels were obliterated by a hellish thunderclap. The rich green mansions of the valley crumbled into dust. His mouth fell open as he looked across a great barren wasteland of smoke and fire, alive with the shrieks and screams of pitiful beings writhing in excruciating, perpetual agony.

The old man sobbed as he fell to his knees, "This can't be...."

"Heaven?" cackled the Devil fiendishly as he plucked the old man's soul from his dead body and cast it into the flame.

* * *

HANGMAN'S OVERLOOK

Jack Harner could not believe the number of shows on the SyFi Channel that related to the supernatural and haunted houses. He was a scam artist who had always placed ghosts on the same list as the Tooth Fairy, Santa Claus, and the Easter Bunny until he researched the topic on the Internet. When he learned that more than 50 percent of people in the United States believe in "things that go bump in the night," he saw a new opportunity to make some easy money.

Wherever he went from that day forward, he made it a point to refute the existence of ghosts, and if anyone took the bait, he would challenge them to a wager. Since he'd come up with the idea four months ago, he had suckered one or more people into a bet and walked away with money in his pocket eleven times. His winnings to date were $12,525.

To win his bets, he had spent the night in six haunted houses, four graveyards, and one abandoned mental hospital.

To expand his operation further, he began to search the Internet for any reports of supernatural activity or strange occurrences in towns where the potential wager would yield more than the cost of transportation and expenses to that location.

A recent story in the *Daily News Record*, which was the Harrisonburg paper, recounted a series of mysterious disappearances of several townspeople over a number of years at a supposedly haunted place called "Hangman's Overlook." The article stated that during the Civil War, the Union Army had captured a party of Confederate soldiers and hanged them at the top of a cliff that overlooked a large part of the Shenandoah Valley. Jack saw this as an excellent opportunity for wagering and was not daunted by the 200-mile trip.

Jack was so excited by the article; he invited Ed Rhodes, an old army buddy who was down on his luck, to join him in the scam to recruit patsies. Ed, who lived in Roanoke, was to receive 25 percent of the profits and a round-trip train ticket to Harrisonburg for his assistance.

After driving into town at about 8:30 in the morning, Jack went to the local eatery, Lloyd's Steakhouse, to wait for Ed, who was arriving at about 8:45 on the train.

After he had nursed several cups of coffee, he saw Ed come in and take a seat at the bar with a copy of the newspaper. While Ed was waiting for his breakfast to be served, he started reading the story aloud to the waitress about the disappearances at the overlook. He read so loud that everyone at the adjoining tables could hear what he was saying and were particularly interested since the topic had received so much media attention.

"A young couple, Curtis Barb and Bonnie Tayman, went to the overlook to park on March eighteenth," Ed recounted as he stirred his cup of coffee. "They were never heard from again. The sheriff and his volunteers combed the area for a week, and now a month later, no trace of the couple has been found."

"Me and my hubby, Homer, used to go up there and park in our courtin' days," the little blonde waitress remembered. "It sure was a spooky place all right. The wind used to howl something awful."

Ed cited five other instances from the local paper's story where other men and women had told their friends that they were headed for the overlook and were never heard from again.

Jack roared with laughter at Ed's account and said for every one to hear, "There no such thing as ghosts and nothing supernatural was responsible for what happened to those people. Only a fool would say a ghost was responsible."

Jack eyed the patsies as he waited for Ed to start the script he'd emailed to him the night before. He wondered how realistically he would deliver the lines.

"Have you ever been to the overlook yourself?" Ed said to Jack, pretending they were strangers.

"No, I'm just a traveler who stopped by for a cup of coffee and some breakfast. I don't even know where Hangman's Overlook is. I only know that people who believe in ghosts are idiots."

Some of the patrons glared at Jack with a look of fire and brimstone.

"I challenge you to go up there at midnight and stand where those soldiers were hanged. I've been there, and I can tell you there's something evil about the place," Ed said eerily.

"Bullshit!" Jack bellowed.

Ed looked at him in mock disbelief and continued, "It gives me the creeps just thinking about how the trees look up there. The sound of the wind blowing across the mountain is like nothing I've ever heard. I remember the strange sounds that came from the bushes and the rocks that made my blood run cold. A pack of something was shrieking and growling."

"What do you mean 'something'?" What kind of animal was it?" Jack inquired sarcastically.

"That's what I mean. It didn't sound like any animal I know of in these parts. Whatever it was, it wasn't human."

Jack finally made his play to pick up some extra cash. "I think your story is bullshit. If you give me two hundred dollars, I'll spend the entire night at the overlook."

"I'll make the wager, but I won't return to the overlook," Ed said solemnly.

"Are there any takers on my bet to spend all night at the overlook?"

A man from a table in the corner scrambled up to the counter and put $200 on the bar and said, "You're on. Me and the boys are going in."

After several others came to the counter with various amounts of money, Jack agreed to wager $1,000 to spend the night at Hangman's Overlook. His ploy had worked like a charm.

The next evening, a small party of spectators in a station wagon and an El Camino met Jack at the overlook as the sun was going down. The small group took their places around the cars and two benches that were located in a picnic area a safe distance from the overlook and started drinking beer. Several had brought binoculars to watch Jack until the sun was completely down. One had night-vision glasses—the kind used on *Ghost Hunters* on the SyFi Network—to be sure he didn't sneak away before daybreak. There were a few rifles leaning against the cars and a handgun on the fender.

After a time, the wind began to howl like a pack of wolves, and Jack heard strange sounds coming from the terrain that was pitch black. He turned on his flashlight and lit a cigarette to settle his nerves.

Jack felt very confident that he was in no danger from the supernatural, but he was a little antsy about the possibility of a psychopath or a wild animal lurking about in the bushes. After all, a number of people had actually disappeared at the overlook according to the article. He felt relieved that he was not alone, and there were seven armed men watching him at a safe distance.

After an hour had passed, Jack made a campfire to lessen the chill of the howling wind. At about midnight he started dancing and singing and carrying on around the campfire like a wild Indian. As the night wore on, the group of spectators were becoming more and more pissed that they were all going to lose their money in the morning. All the scary things that Ed Rhodes had talked about were not happening. By about 4:00, most of the men were shitfaced and dozing and were no longer paying attention to what Jack was doing.

At around 5:30 a.m., the first glint of dawn colored the horizon. Jack was dying for a cigarette and left the overlook and went out to where the two cars were parked. As he approached, he became very uneasy since there was not a sound coming from either car.

He turned on his flashlight and saw blood splattered across the picnic benches and puddles of blood standing in little ditches all around the two cars. There were empty beer cans, McDonald's bags, and spent cigarette buts littering the area around the cars and the blood splatter, but no people.

Jack's eyes flitted to and fro in case the murderers were planning to waste him next, when his eyes fell upon a hodgepodge of bloody bodies piled in the bed of the El Camino. He saw a yellow raincoat on the ground splattered with blood and a machete leaning against the fender. He was about to make a run for it to his car, when he heard a familiar voice from the open window of the second car.

"We're splitting up the money now," Ed Rhodes shouted as he opened the car door and looked at Jack. "We'll have your share shortly."

With his mouth agape, Jack stood in shock surveying the dead bodies, not understanding what had transpired. He saw another man in the car looking toward him as Ed counted a group of bills in the glow of the ceiling light. The headlights of the car came on and shone across the eerie landscape of the overlook.

Momentarily, Ed left the station wagon and joined Jack. He was grinning from ear to ear as he started to explain. "I met this guy on the train to Harrisonburg, and I told him about the wager. He said he had a better idea on how to make a lot more money than $800. He was right. These seven farmers had a grand total of $2,100 in their pockets. And get this; he even knows where there's a swamp nearby to ditch the cars and the bodies."

"You stupid bastard," Jack said as he stared into the muzzle of the twelve-gauge shotgun the stranger was pointing at them.

* * *

THE BOY WHO CRIED "BOOGEYMAN"

I could feel a shiver crawling up my spine as I saw the house where I lived when I was ten years old loom in the distance. My hands were trembling on the steering wheel as I recalled the hideous face of the boogeyman who came to eat me every night when it got dark twenty-five years ago.

Before I left New York, I emailed one of the friends to find out if the house was still standing. I was excited to find out when he responded that the house was not only standing, it was for sale; consequently, I made prior arrangements with a realtor to show me the house at 5 p.m. today.

Now that I was here, I didn't know how I would react when I went inside. The memories returned with a vengeance as I remembered the horror I had experienced so many years ago.

The one-story, white frame house was surrounded by grass. It needed a paint job, but otherwise it was just the way I remembered it. The trailer park that was located behind the property also rekindled memories. I remembered the eight-year-old kid that told me how babies were made and the teenagers that had caused me to crash my bicycle.

I blamed my parents for not believing the boogeyman lived in my closet, but in retrospect, I wondered what I would have done in their place? They hadn't ignored my pleas for help at first. They came running into my room in the middle of the night many times and found nothing out of the ordinary. After weeks of false alarms, they finally stopped coming to my rescue and just yelled, "Go to sleep. There's no such thing as the boogeyman."

After I knew they would not get involved, I begged them to leave the light on in my room when I went to bed, but they said it would increase the electric bill for no reason.

I found a flashlight in the kitchen drawer that I kept with me under the covers each night, but up to that time, I had never used it. When my parents turned out the light in my bedroom, I simply pulled the sheet and sometimes the blanket over my head to keep from being eaten during the night. I never understood why my sheet protected me, but it always did.

Once at breakfast, my parents asked me to tell them what my monster looked like. I told them I had never seen him in the daytime. He only came out after dark when they had gone to bed. Every night I heard the closet door creak open and his foot dragging across the floor toward my bed. When the streetlights came on outside, I could see his silhouette in the window standing over me, poised to strike if I left the protection of my sheet.

I pleaded with my parents to let me sleep in their bedroom, but they wouldn't hear of it. The boogeyman was smart; he wanted to get me alone. He could not eat me up when my parents were with me or when the lights were on. These were the rules I lived by every day and every night I was in this dreaded house.

Once I went to my school library and looked up the word in an encyclopedia to see what could keep such a monster at bay or what could kill it. Unlike a stake through the heart for a vampire and a silver bullet for a werewolf, the encyclopedia didn't say how to kill a boogeyman.

During the last month I lived in the house, I finally caught a glimpse of him when I had to go to the bathroom and couldn't wait for morning. When I could hold it no longer, I turned on the flashlight and pointed it at his face. To my amazement, he was momentarily blinded. I gathered up my sheets and my blanket and threw them at him as I ran for my life from my room into the bathroom. In the split second the flashlight was on him, I saw his claw like fingers on the bed post, a mouthful of long pointed teeth, and two snakelike eyes glaring at me. Since I dared not return to my room until morning, I had to sleep on the sofa in the living room for the rest of the night.

My parents rolled their eyes when I told them what had happened at breakfast, and I drew a picture of what I had seen in hopes they would finally believe me. That evening after dinner, my mother read me a story from a book she had gotten at the library titled *The Boy Who Cried Wolf*. It was useless; they still didn't believe me.

I was so happy when my father got a new job, and we moved away from that dreadful place—never to return.

My new home didn't have a boogeyman. In fact, none of the houses I lived in during my adult life had one. I never forgot what had happened then, but I never talked about it to anyone since I knew they would say, "There is no such thing as the boogeyman."

As I pulled my Mercedes into the driveway at the back entrance to the house, I saw a man hammering a new "for sale" sign in the grass on the front lawn. I got out of my car and approached him.

"Are you Mr. Payne from Mt. Vernon Realty? I'm John Green, the one who called to see the house. I lived here until I was ten years old many years ago."

The man smiled and shook my hand, which was abnormally cold to the touch, and said warmly, "Yes, I am Tom Payne, and if you like the house, I think you can buy it for an unbelievable price."

"There are so many memories from so long ago (All bad, I thought without saying). I can't wait to see my old room and the rest of the house. It seems like yesterday I cut the grass for my father."

"The owners have instructed me to have a crew come out next week to give the house a new coat of paint. Try to imagine this improvement as we do the walk-through."

"Would you mind very much if my initial walk-through is by myself? I really want to take my time in each room."

"No problem. Whenever you're ready, I'm here to answer any questions you might have."

"Thank you so much." I said as a strange familiarity tickled my senses as we approached the house. "I hate to admit it, but I was very afraid of the boogeyman when I lived here, and I am hoping that some of my old anxieties will be relieved once I see my room as an adult."

I thought he was going to tell me, "There's no such thing as a boogeyman," but he ignored the comment and proceeded to the front porch.

As the realtor and I approached the front door, I noticed he had an awkward gait. He couldn't seem to lift his left foot from the ground. He unlocked the large white door and, after opening it, showed me the living room. Afterward, complying with my request, he shuffled through the kitchen and took a seat on the back porch.

To my amazement, the living room was almost the same as I remembered. There, inside the door, was the piano my mother had played when I was a boy. I had forgotten all about it since it was not in the house we bought after this one. The other pieces of furniture seemed familiar in the positions they occupied in the room, but the small-screen television I had watched *Gunsmoke* and my other favorite shows on had been replaced with a new flat-screen television.

A second feeling of déjà vu crept over me as I went into the kitchen. I remembered the time I wrote "shit" in soap on the kitchen window on the night before Halloween. My mother thought some of the kids that lived in the trailer park had sneaked into our yard and soaped the window. I never told her I did it.

When I returned to the kitchen, I noticed the realtor was no longer on the back porch.

I continued my tour and inspected my parents' bedroom and also the third bedroom. Both rooms seemed very similar to the way they had been when I lived here.

My initial pang of trepidation returned as I walked toward the room where the boogeyman and I lived so long ago. Taking a deep breath, I pushed open the door and timidly inched inside. My eyes surveyed the four walls that had given me so many sleepless and terrifying nights. The closet door was closed as I approached it. My hand trembled as I put it on the doorknob and opened it with apprehension. A loud creak startled me as I stepped back at the ready for something to spring from the closet upon me. Nothing moved from within as I peered inside.

There were clothes on the hanger and a number of boxes on the shelves. I pulled a cord, which turned on an overhead light. Everything inside was washed in the glow of a 100-watt bulb. There was nothing foreboding about the interior of the closet. I looked back at the room and turned on the overhead light with a switch on the wall. The room was cheerful and neat without any ominous overtones.

I heaved a sigh of relief and sat on the bed. It seemed that the rules had not changed regarding the boogeyman. In the window, I saw the sun fading through the trees and the sky turning dark. I remembered what that had meant when I lived here.

I lay back on the bed and rested my head on the pillow. With deep concentration, I tried to bring back the way I felt as a child. I had never experienced anything since that felt more real than the monster that lived in my closet when I was ten.

Were my parents and all the others right all along? I was still convinced they were not. I remembered his insidious laughter in the closet, the foot dragging across the floor, and those hideous pointed teeth. The house was still and extremely creepy, but I assumed that no one but myself would feel the vibes that I was feeling at that moment.

I arose from the bed and left the room with a shudder and a lump in my throat. I gave the kitchen one last look and noticed the butcher knives in a rack on the wall. I thought about the damage someone could do with those as I ventured out on the screened back porch and down the steps into the backyard.

The realtor was standing with his back to me digging a hole in the ground next to the garage. I followed the sidewalk to the separate structure and joined him. On the ground along the garage wall was a series of five small white crosses in what appeared to be a flower garden next to a line of rosebushes. On the horizontal slat of each cross was a name and a date. They read in the order of their position: "John, 1965;" "Patrick, 1975;" Henry, 1985;" "Sydney, 1995;" and "Aidan, 2005."

"What do you make of these markers?" I said incredulously.

"One of the neighbors thought that these are graves of some of the pets that lived here through the years." The realtor looked at the sky and the sun going down.

"The names don't look like pet names to me. I lived here in 1965, and my name is John, but I'm certainly not buried here, and we didn't have any pets."

The realtor smiled and took another shovelful of dirt from the flower garden as he looked at his watch and said, "I only know what I was told, but one thing's for sure, the crosses aren't a good selling point. I want to make this area a flower bed rather than a pet cemetery."

"How long did the last owner live here?" I inquired as the sun descended to the bottom of the horizon and shadows of branches fell across the garage wall.

"As I understand it, he was here for about ten years. The neighbors say that his little boy had disturbing nightmares all the time he lived here. Then one day when he didn't answer their call for breakfast, they found what was left of him scattered about his bedroom floor. The police said the forensics indicated the he was killed by some kind of animal. The strange part was there was no sign of forced entry or exit and no conclusive identification of what kind of animal it was. The owners were so distraught they moved out that day and put the house on the market the next week. That was five years ago. We've reduced the price to the point where we're giving the house away, but there have been no takers."

The realtor turned to me and said, "Would you be in the market? You and your parents lived here before, and nothing happened to you. In fact, I lived in this house myself for a time, and I never had a problem."

I took a step back as I pondered his last remark and said, "I'm sorry to say, after so many bad memories, I wouldn't live in this house if you gave it to me and threw in an extra million dollars to boot."

"Do you still think there's a boogeyman in your closet?"

"I don't remember mentioning that he lived in my closet."

"Don't all boogeymen live in closets?"

I smiled uneasily and said, "I understand in some countries they live under the bed."

Some of the lights in the neighboring condos came on, and a cool breeze caught the back of my neck as my heartbeat began to accelerate.

Looking back at the house, I asked, "Why would one case of a random animal attack stop the house from selling for five years at such a reduced price?"

"Apparently, there were several other deaths before this one. The straw that broke the camel's back was when the *Alexandria Gazette* ran an article, which listed the dates and the children who died going back to when the house was built. Since the story was printed, no one wants to buy the house at any price."

"It's apparent you should change your line of work. You'll never sell this house if you tell potential buyers that story."

The realtor dragged his left foot and shuffled toward the "for sale" sign, and pulling it out of the ground, he propped it against the back porch out of sight from the road.

"I'm not really the realtor. I made a meal of him last night when he came to air out the house," the boogeyman said cloaked in darkness.

I looked at the shape-shifting silhouette against the deep purple hue of the sky and didn't understand how my former nocturnal roommate could be outside of his closet, particularly before sundown. It was another boogeyman rule omitted from the encyclopedia and one more thing to worry about if my plan was to conclude the way I had planned.

A half moon rose eerily behind the trees and two street lights came on as I saw his face morph into something inhuman with long pointed teeth and his body contort into the familiar shape of my former roommate.

I retreated up the stairs into the house and into my old room. I pulled back the sheets and got into bed the same as I did when I was ten years old. It wasn't long before I heard the familiar sound of his foot dragging across the floor and I heard a deep raspy voice say, "I've been waiting for you, Johnnie. I knew you would come back to see me."

"Mom! Dad! The boogieman is trying to eat me!" I screamed.

"Your parents aren't here to save you this time. You're all alone, and the dark is so beautiful," said the boogeyman.

On queue, John's parents, who were both sixty-five years old, stepped into his room and turned on the light. For the first time, they caught a glimpse of the monster as he fled into his closet in dismay.

"Mom! Dad! Do you believe me now?"

"Yes, son. We saw him with our own eyes," his parents' confirmed in unison.

"Sorry we didn't believe you all those years ago," his father said and then asked, "Did you make all of the arrangements?"

"Yes, Dad, I am now the proud owner of this house. I bought it this morning for thirty thousand dollars. The bank was giving it away as a foreclosure."

"You sure went out on a limb, son. What if the boogeyman wasn't here?"

"In my heart, I knew he would be, and I knew he would be coming to eat me just as before when it got dark."

I saw several members of the local fire department pull up in a fire truck in the driveway.

I left the lights ablaze in my room and went outside to instruct the fire department to begin torching my new house as I had arranged earlier.

My parents and I got in my car and drove off as the flames from my old house set the night on fire.

Torching the house closed the door on the boogeyman forever. It was the most satisfying $30,000 I ever spent.

* * *

WEREWOLF ON BROADWAY

The receptionist finally called Marlowe to see Mr. Abramson, a promoter who had orchestrated the careers of Elvis, the Beatles, and many other lesser mortals. After she escorted him into an expansive executive office overlooking Central Park, he took a chair facing the promoter and shuffled his feet nervously.

"Mr. Marlowe," Abramson cracked the ice, "I don't usually meet someone without a track record, but a friend of a friend who I respect thought you had an act which has a lot of potential. Please elaborate."

"I know you are a busy man, and I'll get right to the point. I am a werewolf. My idea is to have you set up a show on Broadway with a number of other acts, which will be a vehicle for me to display my unique talent to a packed house of spectators and make lots of money."

Abramson's jaw dropped and he sat dumbfounded for a few seconds, and then with an exasperated look on his face, he picked up the phone to call for security.

"I assure you I am not a crackpot. I am willing to give you a demonstration of my act on November fifteenth, which will be the next full moon."

The promoter paused with the phone to his ear and put the receiver back down.

"Is this some kind of gimmick where you transform into a werewolf with smoke and mirrors? We both know that werewolves don't exist."

"I don't blame you for being skeptical, but I assure you there's no smoke and mirrors," Marlowe explained. "The act will be authentic. You are also wrong about the existence of werewolves. In point of fact, my father is a werewolf. The difference between myself and the others is that I don't prey on humans. Except for the night of each full moon, I live a pretty normal life. I am confident that I am the only werewolf in existence that can make that claim."

"How are you able to avoid ripping people apart when the moon is full and," he said melodramatically, "the wolf bane blooms."

"My father has sheltered me all my life from the bestial inclination to hunt and devour humans for food, which had been his unfortunate plight for two hundred years. Since childhood I have adhered to his strict demands to avoid the curse. On the day of the full moon, I am placed in a padded cell that keeps me at bay, and I am served a bloody feast of raw animal meat to satisfy my hunger until my lust for blood and my transformation passes. A human who befriended my father did the same for him until he died."

Marlowe could see Abramson coming around and was actually surprised that he had not dismissed the concept entirely. It was likely that most nonbelievers would not entertain the existence of a real werewolf whatsoever.

After pausing to collect his thoughts, he added, "My father was very fortunate that circumstances allowed him to acquire substantial wealth. This enabled him to hire professional bodyguards to provide for our captivity and feeding during each full moon."

Abramson looked at Marlowe, and although he thought his story defied any stretch of the imagination, he had the uncanny feeling he was telling the truth. He knew by his demeanor that he believed what he was saying, and if he wasn't a complete mental fruitcake, this was a once-in-a-lifetime opportunity. It was like finding another Elvis.

Marlowe explained, "I got the idea when I saw *King Kong* on the tube a few weeks ago. In the movie, an American film crew, led by Carl Denim, captured 'Kong,' a giant prehistoric gorilla, and brought him in chains to New York City to be exhibited as the Eighth Wonder of the World. Every show was sold out until Kong broke through his chains and wasted a lot of ticket holders and most of Times Square. I can take Kong's place as the Eighth Wonder of the World, and we can make millions."

"Millions," Abramson repeated in a daze.

The promoter rose from his desk, peered out across New York City, and watched the masses flitting about like ants on the streets below. He tried to curb his excitement and said as he faced Marlowe, "Look. It sounds good, but we need to schedule a viewing of your transformation before I proceed with anything. It's sounds too good to be true, and if I can't get my mind around it, how can I promote it?"

"As I said, November fifteenth, which is next Friday, the moon will be full, and you can come to my father's compound on Riverside Drive and watch me turn into a werewolf."

"How many full moons are there in a year?" The promoter asked.

"Always twelve, some years thirteen."

Abramson was disappointed, but twelve sellout shows at Madison Square Garden was a big haul by anybody's standard if he played his cards right. He thought of putting together some Cirque du Soleil–type acts, a rock group for the kids, and maybe the Rockettes for the old farts with Marlowe's Werewolf transformation—the main event.

The days passed, and finally November 15 came. Abramson and an entourage drove up in stretch limos and parked in the large circular driveway on Riverside Drive. The sun was fading on the horizon. It was about a half an hour before sundown. The chauffer went to the door and rang the doorbell, and a tall mountain of a man that looked like a wrestler answered the door and ushered them inside a large foyer with a huge crystal chandelier.

"Follow me," he instructed the group of eight and led them down a dimly lit stairway that led to the basement.

In the room below was a huge cage with very large bars that appeared to be made of steel. Marlowe sat on the one chair inside the enclosure. A steer was tied to one of the bars in one corner of the space.

Ten chairs were lined up in a row in front of the cage. Abramson and his group took a seat. There was an unpleasant smell surrounding the space like spoiled meat, and the hay that was strewn about the floor was clotted with blood and gore.

A huge monitor on the wall showed the full moon rising in the sky from an outside video feed. A strain of creepy pipe organ music crept into the space from the speakers that were positioned around the cage. Marlowe's face suddenly filled the monitor as the intensity of the soundtrack grew louder and the bass speakers shook the enclosure.

Before their horror-stricken eyes, Marlowe transformed into a colossal hairy beast, half man and half animal. The eyes of the wolf man filled with ravenous hunger as he looked out at the party of eight. With all his might he attempted to break free of the steel cage. The bars held. With no recourse, he pounced upon the steer and started tearing the animal to bits one limb at a time. The ferocity and the unbridled bloodlust were much more primitive than any film the spectators had ever seen. The vicious slaughter made *Blood Feast* look like a Disney cartoon. The smell and the splatter of blood that sprayed inside and through the bars caused all eight spectators to gag and vomit violently. After devouring his pray, the wolf man returned to his chair and watched the group outside the cage with such terrifying menace that the two women who had come with Abramson passed out from fright and slumped to the ground. After several minutes, Marlowe burped loudly and started to transform back into his human form.

After becoming human once again, he picked up a blood-splattered robe, draped it around himself, and said to the group, "Wasn't I fantastic?" Blood and gore was caked on his face, and slivers of meat hung from his incisors.

Abramson gave him an affirmative nod as several bodyguards helped him to his feet and up the stairs to the outside. His entourage was splattered with blood as they stood in the driveway gasping for breath from the excruciating ordeal.

By the next full moon, a magnificent production was staged at Madison Square Garden. The seating capacity for the show was 20,000 at $300 per ticket for the cheap seats and $2,000 for the seats directly in front of the stage. Four Cirque du Soleil acts, the Rockettes, and Kiss were the acts that preceded the main event, *Marlowe-Werewolf on Broadway.* All the tickets were sold out within a week, and the show was the talk of the entertainment world. Massive TV screens circled the stage in order for all in attendance to witness the carnage in what Abramson was advertising as "Horrorvision."

The spectators in the front-row seats were given "splatter coats" and damp hand towels to cleanse their face and hands. The entire audience was given plastic vomit bags for those who became queasy. Fresh air was pumped through the air conditioning units, and exhaust fans were twirling like helicopter blades to soften the stench of the bodily fluids during the show.

As expected, the event more than lived up to the massive ad campaign. Many of the spectators passed out and had to be removed from the theater on stretchers. The police had their hands full with the unruly crowd that seemed to relish every shower of blood like they were seeing Gallagher, the comedian, splatter the audience with watermelon juice. The front-row yellow splatter coats were soaked in scarlet, and people were slipping and sliding in the unbridled pandemonium.

Abramson wanted to take the show to larger venues to increase the gate, but he feared that a larger arena would diminish the thrill of the slaughter.

After two years, the audiences started to subside and the promoter needed to rejuvenate the show. New supporting acts were not enough.

Abramson called a meeting with Marlowe and his father at his mansion in Greenwich.

Marlowe and his father lit up two Cuban cigars that were offered to them and sipped on Remy Martin's Black Pearl cognac when the promoter opened the meeting. "*Werewolf on Broadway* has been an incredibly successful enterprise, and we replenished the funds you were initially after to continue your lifestyle for years to come."

Marlowe and his father smiled with pride and took another puff on their cigars.

"However, I want to double the take on the show with a new angle, and I need your help to pull it off."

After what you have done for us, we would be happy to do whatever you think would increase the show's popularity.

"We need to turn a real werewolf loose in New York City. I suggest the red-light district would be the most advantageous for the media. It will make headlines like Jack the Ripper. Can you call up one of your werewolf friends and tell them to rip a few prostitutes apart on the next full moon?"

Marlowe looked at the promoter in disbelief and said defiantly, "My father and I want no part of such an insidious plot. We are happy with the current results."

Abramson hit a button on his desk, and eight beefy strongmen entered the room and grabbed Marlowe and his father and escorted them to a padded cell in the basement. The massive steel doors slammed shut like a bank vault.

The promoter spoke into a microphone, and the two prisoners heard his voice resonating from the ceiling. "Our partnership has ended. From now on you will do what I say if you want to continue not being like all the other werewolves."

"You wouldn't do that. I beg you not to. What kind of monster are you?"

"You're the monster, not me." Abramson snickered. "I promote big box office attractions, and you are it. I got the idea from watching *King Kong* last night. Carl Denim didn't share his profits with the big ape, he simply put him in a cell until show time."

During the next full moon, the promoter's men turned Marlowe's father loose in the red-light district. He had not eaten for several days and was ravenous. As the night progressed, he brutally devoured three prostitutes and left the pieces of their body strewn about the streets. The police sirens were blaring continuously while Marlowe was the main event at the Garden. The promoter's cronies followed Marlowe's father and even watched the carnage with the prostitutes. Once his blood lust was satisfied and he returned to human form, they fell upon him with a stun gun and returned him to his cell.

Several months passed, and Abramson received a proposition from ten Saudi oil barons that they would pay handsomely to see a special show where several young women were placed in the cage with Marlowe rather than the steer. They offered to pay five million dollars to film the werewolf devouring the three young women, who were to be purchased on the black market in Mexico.

Abramson agreed to the terms and made arrangements for the special show to follow the Garden show at his home in Greenwich.

As planned, after the main event at the Garden, Marlowe was taken in chains in a Brinks truck to Abramson's mansion. A small auditorium was set up with the steel cage with fifty seats for spectators. Oil barons filled about half of the seats and the promoter and his men filled the rest.

The full moon hung suspended in the sky as several of Abramson's stooges went into the cage and started beating Marlowe with a bullwhip until his anger caused him to begin his transformation into a wolf for the second time that evening. The men exited the cage and took a seat in the audience. From high above the stage, a scantily clad young woman with enormous breasts, who was chained to a platform, was lowered into the cage from above. A film director screamed commands to various members of the crew that began filming the event from eight different vantage points around the stage. Creepy music began to build as Marlowe glared at the women's body stretched across the platform. Strobe lights began to pulse as the room lights dimmed, and spotlights filled the interior of the cage.

Suddenly unbridled shrieks and screams filled the room, not from the cage, but from the audience, as the house lights flooded the entire interior. The camera crew swiveled their cameras toward the oil barons and at Abramson and his henchmen. About half of the Saudi's had been ripped apart by a pack of werewolves who were making their rounds in the audience. The yellow blood-splatter slickers the spectators were wearing were becoming drenched with their own blood as the sound of gnashing teeth and breaking bones filled the room. Abramson was escorted in chains into the cage to face Marlowe, who had been joined by his father.

Marlowe ripped a piece of flesh from the promoter's cheek and popped it into his bloody mouth. Abramson was sobbing violently and begging for mercy as Marlowe continued to slice off bits of meat from his paunchy jowls with his long claws and explained, "Let me introduce a few more members of my family who are all werewolves that have lived undercover for a hundred years."

The sound of sucking and slurping continued as Marlowe's brothers and sisters continued to devour all the spectators, but the promoter.

"Three years ago, our sister, Rosy, was slaughtered in one of your snuff movies. We developed the *Werewolf on Broadway* ruse to flush out the Saudi bastards who paid you to make the film. Finally, we have our revenge for her death and a considerable amount of money to boot."

Marlowe's father began chewing on Abramson's right ear as Marlowe skewered his eyeball like an olive with his index claw. Blood sprayed across the promoter's lips as Marlowe, savoring each morsel, said, "We purposely saved you for last. After all the pain and suffering you have caused our family, we really have a bone to pick with you."

* * *

THE BABYSITTER

The sun disappeared behind the trees as the bonfire was ignited. Hundreds of high school students were getting ready for a pep-rally. Mount Vernon was coming to play the Eagles on Saturday. The cheerleaders were getting into position to perform their first cheer as Lisa Sloan, a very bad seed, climbed the bleachers and found a seat among the spectators who were beginning to assemble from all directions. Her winter coat was shabby, and she didn't seem the type to care about football.

"Who are we fooling?" Lisa mused. The Eagles were going to be obliterated all over the field come Saturday. She looked at the candy-ass quarterback flirting with all the girls with big boobs while his homecoming queen honey was busy turning cartwheels with the cheerleaders. His perfect teeth were sparkling in the firelight. God, how she loathed his kind. She thought of how much fun it would be to run over his ass.

Lisa was a loner. Her old lady had run off with some loser, and the cash she saved as a waitress the previous summer was almost gone. Going to school was a waste of time, and she hated everything about it. Education was not going to make a big difference in her life. The only jobs she could look forward to were dead-end jobs like those her mother always had. She wasn't going to marry someone who was born with a silver spoon. Few men were drawn to her for anything but a quick piece of ass. The only real girlfriend she ever had was cleaning up turning tricks in Vegas, and Lisa wanted a piece of that action.

She lit a cigarette and contemplated how she was going to get her traveling money together and kick the dust of this crummy town off her worn-out Reeboks.

Two prim and proper female geeks climbed the bleachers and sat down nearby. She could throw up just listening to them talking. The taller girl moved a little bit farther away when she spotted Lisa, but Lisa could still hear them blabbering.

"I'm going to Europe with my folks for a whole month," said Stephanie, "and the Pidcocks are going to need a substitute babysitter. Do you think you'd be interested?"

"Pidcock? Are those the people who live in that huge mansion up on Knob Hill?" Maria questioned.

"The same, and they pay twelve dollars an hour."

"I guess that must mean their little brat is a real monster," Maria said sarcastically.

"Not at all, Matthew is the sweetest little boy I've ever babysat for."

"Sounds too good to be true, but tell the Pidcocks they've found their new babysitter. When do they need me?"

"Saturday night, seven o'clock," Stephanie remarked, pulling her wool coat tighter around her neck as the winter wind whistled across the bleachers.

"Perfect," Maria chimed as she winced from another gust of bitter-cold wind.

The two young girls kept looking back at Lisa like she had the plague and finally got up and descended the bleachers to get closer to the bonfire and away from her. Lisa glared at them in disgust, but kept watching them laughing and making small talk. If looks could kill, they would have been dead meat. She had never seen them before, but hoped she would see them again in some dark alley when she was wielding a chain saw. The school was so large it was hard to really know anyone except the students in your own classes.

Lisa saw a piece of paper fall from a stack of books one of them was carrying as the girls walked away. Neither of them noticed it. Lisa waited. After they were out of sight, she picked up the paper and realized it had all the information she had heard them discussing: names, addresses, and telephone numbers of the bitches and Mr. and Mrs. Pidcock. This was too good to be true. Lady Luck was smiling on her at last. This was the opportunity she had been waiting for.

Lisa continued to think about what they had said. Those stupid bitches didn't know she had heard everything. Now she had all the information she needed to get inside the Pidcock mansion and take as much as she could carry. Lisa was smiling from ear to ear as she left the fire and the fanfare behind and headed home.

She loved trouble and was always on the take. Shoplifting had been a way of life for her since she was seven. Her mother had taught her the ropes and she felt a rush every time she left a store with the goods. She had even sold drugs to eleven-year-olds to make a buck until her contact dried up. Did she care that she may have ruined their lives or that because of her they may have become addicts for life? Everybody has a cross of some kind to bear. These rich kids had too much money for their own good.

Most comfortable in a black leather motorcycle jacket, Lisa was the first in all her classes to sport a huge spider tattoo on her upper arm. When she really wanted to mess somebody up, she always loved the snap, crackle, and pop of a good baseball bat. She had made her living stealing from derelicts that inhabited the alleys in her part of town. Ever since she saw *A Clockwork Orange*, she had never taken prisoners, and she'd never been caught.

She couldn't imagine how much easy loot—silver, diamonds— could be lying around that big house on Knob Hill. She had to do a little homework to come up with a dress suitable for such a special occasion. She hated the rich with a passion and never dreamed such a grand opportunity would arise for her to do a little number on them and garner some road money at the same time. It was going to be like taking candy from a baby.

She hadn't anticipated having this much fun since she poisoned old Mrs. Hearn's dog and drowned her four cats in North River last month.

The week passed, and Lisa stole most of what she needed to impersonate a respectable member of the teen community.

At five o'clock Saturday night, Maria received the call from Lisa, pretending to be Mrs. Pidcock. "I'm really sorry to have to call you at this late hour to tell you that my husband is very ill with the flu, and we have to cancel our plans for this evening. We are truly sorry for the inconvenience and want to compensate you the next time you babysit, which, I hope, could be next Saturday, if possible."

"I'm really sorry that Mr. Pidcock is sick, and I understand entirely about canceling this evening. I'm looking forward to babysitting for you next Saturday. Would that still be at seven?"

"Yes, that would be fine."

"You'll pick me up right outside my house, like we planned this evening?"

"That will be perfect. Again, I'm truly sorry to cancel so late. I hope you can still make other plans for this evening."

"Don't worry, Mrs. Pidcock. My mom and dad are going to the movies in a little while, and I'll probably join them," Maria answered.

"See you next Saturday."

Lisa was so excited. Everything was working so well.

At ten minutes to seven, Lisa drove by Maria's house in her old Chevy and parked around the corner out of sight. There was a light on the front porch and a light inside, but it appeared that no one was stirring. She strolled up to the front of the house to wait for Mrs. Pidcock.

At exactly seven o'clock, a new Mercedes pulled up with a sophisticated looking lady, apparently dressed to go to a very elegant affair.

Lisa approached the car. "Hello, Mrs. Pidcock, I'm Maria. I'm so happy to finally meet you and to be your babysitter for this evening. Stephanie has told me so much about you and your husband and what an angel Matthew is."

The wealthy bitch was overwhelmed by her charm and believed everything she had said without question. It was fortunate that Mrs. Pidcock couldn't see the tattoos under her clothing and was so trusting toward someone she had never met.

Lisa lied about her courses at school and said she was looking forward to college and a career in publishing. She laughed to herself: The closest she'd ever get to publishing would be the latest issue of *Road Warrior* or posing for a low-class skin magazine.

The Mercedes wound up the long circular driveway leading to the entrance of the sprawling mansion. Lisa's eyes glittered in the glow of the magnificent chandelier that hung in the foyer. The expanse of the interior was awesome to her as she looked to the left and right. A huge painting of a medieval castle hung high on a large wall, and the ceiling seemed to climb several stories above the entryway. She didn't want to appear overly impressed, but it was hard to hide her excitement and wonder.

Almost at once, Mr. Pidcock joined his wife in the foyer, looking polished and impeccably dressed. He introduced himself and looked her over at first a little cautiously, then led her into another immense room with a mammoth television.

Mrs. Pidcock showed her the kitchen and, most particularly, the refrigerator. She told her to make herself comfortable and to help herself to anything she wanted in the way of refreshments. The pantry was filled with every kind of snack imaginable. And then in a flurry, Matthew scurried in carrying four large balloons, which he swirled about like he was about to fly a kite.

Mrs. Pidcock proudly said, "This is Matthew. He is eight years old and loves to play games. He goes to bed about nine-thirty or ten. He's usually no bother. That's what Stephanie always said."

"Hello, Matthew. It's very nice to meet you!" exclaimed Lisa with her most precious smile.

Matthew seemed very shy and looked up at her with brown eyes that seemed too big for his head. He stared into her eyes and in the sweetest little voice said, "Hello, Maria, I'm very pleased to meet you. Do you like games? I'm very good at games!"

"I love games," Lisa offered as she thought of the various types of pain she might inflict on this little Lord Fauntleroy.

The parents showed her around a little more, gave her some more instructions on what to do in their absence, and with a minimum of ceremony, departed into the night for an evening of entertainment. As they drove off, she saw rain dart across the huge picture window facing the driveway and heard the low rumbling of a storm rolling in.

"What game do you want to play first?" a little voice timidly asked as she made sure the coast was clear.

"How about hide and seek?" Lisa suggested.

"Yes! Yes!" screamed Matthew.

"I'm going to count to one hundred pretty slowly to give you time to find a good hiding place, and then I'll try to find you. Why don't you go upstairs and hide? I've got a big surprise for you when I find you. The better you hide and the longer it takes me to find you, the bigger the surprise."

"I love surprises!" chirped Matthew.

"Are you afraid to go upstairs by yourself?"

"No, I'm not afraid," Matthew answered after pondering over the question for a moment. Then, for no reason she could imagine, he looked up at her inquisitively and asked, "Are you a very nice person?"

"I'll let you be the judge of that when the night is over."

"I can't wait to get my hands on you," Lisa mused as Matthew ran off excitedly. She started to count aloud slowly as she found several pillowcases in a hall closet and started accumulating anything that was small and expensive. She checked all the rooms on the first floor and had quite a collection of items in no time.

"Sixty...sixty-one..." Lisa shouted as she made a fast ham and cheese sandwich and downed a Coors Light. She saw a large butcher knife in the rack on the kitchen wall and extracted it. A fiendish grin swept over her face as she thought of the atrocities she might mete out later. She began to move toward the spiral staircase.

She heard a sound high up at the top of the house. The sound was muffled by the great expanse of the home filled with so many beautiful things.

Outside the thunder growled in the evening sky. Fingers of lightning made the crystal chandeliers dim in an eerie and grotesque ambiance. The storm was getting much worse, very fast. Suddenly, a violent thunderclap felt like it had hit the house. Shivers ran up her spine as she climbed the staircase leading to the bedrooms. Each time the thunder crashed, the lights flickered. She wondered how she would ever find the little brat if the lights went out. She hadn't planned on this inconvenience.

A rush of cold air fell from somewhere above as if someone had opened a huge meat locker. The air conditioning was off since it was chilly outside. The sound of rain on the roof grew louder with each ascending step. She shouted to the still darkness above, "One hundred. Here I come, ready or not!"

It seemed like it took forever to finally make it to the top of the stairs. She looked both ways. For a fleeting moment, she recalled Martin Balsam reaching the top of the stairs in *Psycho* as her eyes darted about uneasily. She looked down into the shimmering foyer filled with sparkling crystal and exquisite tapestries, and for that split second, she thought she knew what it must feel like to have it all. So many mixed emotions embraced her at that moment: fear, wonder, anticipation. She had never felt so alive.

She looked both ways once again and decided to go left toward the part of the house where she thought she had heard the muffled sound. Up ahead on both sides of the hallway was a string of meticulously spaced lit candles reminiscent of something she might have seen in a horror flick about witchcraft. The candles hadn't been there when Mrs. Pidcock had shown her Matthew's bedroom. Matthew must have lit them. How mysterious, she thought, for an eight-year-old to be playing with matches.

"Am I getting warmer or colder?" she shouted. There was no answer from the dark silence that lay in the distance behind the candlelight. Between the claps of thunder, the sound of pouring rain echoed through the big house.

A giant bang shook the whole structure as if lightning had hit something very hard. The lights went out. The ponderous "bong" of an ancient clock tolled somewhere below and pounded out eight as the sound of small steps running above pricked her ears.

"I hear you! And I'm coming to get you," Lisa screamed. "Don't be afraid of the dark. Stay where you are, and I'll be right there." The sound of giggling, muffled and distant, made her heart beat faster as she came to another flight of stairs that she thought must lead to the attic.

"I think I know where you are!" Lisa screamed. "I have a big surprise for you, Matthew. Like I promised, a big, big surprise!" Lisa removed the giant butcher knife from her belt and ascended the steps toward a large door at the top of the stairs.

Finally, she put her ear to the door and listened. The noise was very muffled by the big door, but it sounded like an arcade was inside once she got very close. It was like she had come upon a battleground, a sports complex, a circus, a Star Trek adventure, and a carnival all at the same time. Her heart beat faster and faster as she gripped the knife and slowly and silently opened the heavy door.

Across the room was a wall of monitors, each with its own type of video game: Racecars were racing, baseball players running, monsters exploding, pinballs scattering, and spaceships warping. Stationed in front of this wall of screens was a huge command center with a large executive chair that faced away from the entry door.

She inched deeper into the room. "Matthew," she whispered. "I've found you."

One by one, all the screens on the large wall changed to still images of Lisa putting the silver in a pillowcase, ransacking this drawer and that, and holding the giant butcher knife with her eyes wide with excitement. The calliope of nonsense and noise ended abruptly, and an instant void of sound displaced the disjointed roar of the arcade. Lisa's heartbeat accellerated as the giant chair facing the wall of monitors slowly turned toward her. Lisa's eyes glazed in the illumination of the monitors as she stared into the bloodshot eyes of what only minutes before was little Matthew. But now these eyes were not innocent and childlike. They were devilish and cruel. The teeth were pointed, and the lips curled into a ravenous smile.

Two double doors opened on both sides of the room and a weird flapping sound emanated from the black rooms behind the doors. A hideous bat-like thing appeared from the right and like magic turned from a black, winged form into a tall pale man in a tuxedo and black cape. More flapping and more guests dressed in back gowns and capes materialized from chambers beyond. A dank smell rushed in, and a sudden chill swept into the room from the gaping black doorways.

Three beefy vampires in tuxedos grabbed Lisa's arms and twisted the knife from her grasp. Turning her upside down, they carried her screaming to the center of the marble floor and impaled her on a stainless steel meat hook that hung from the ceiling. A massive crystal punch bowl was placed under her head as big band music from the forties began to play.

Mathew's parents and the students who had discussed the babysitting job materialized from the blackness and met little

Matthew at the punch bowl in anticipation of the toast to begin the festivities. She saw their ghastly black eyes in the flickering candlelight as the headwaiter slit her throat with a carving knife. The waiters proceeded to distribute a goblet of blood to each guest from the crystal reservoir.

Except for Lisa, a grand time of dining, dancing, and sparkling conversation was enjoyed by all.

* * *

THE INITIATION

A van of six fraternity brothers pulled up to a tall wooden fence, approximately ten feet high, located in a remote section of the Fort Belvoir Army Base. The night of the long-awaited initiation of the plebes into the Alpha Phi Omega fraternity had finally arrived. Jerry's watch read 8:45 p.m. as he climbed down from the van that was hidden just around the bend from the entrance of the compound and was shielded from view by heavy terrain.

Jerry looked at the others with a shit-eating grin on his face and said, "This is the best idea we've ever had. This will be a night to remember. A hell night to top all hell nights!"

Charlie chuckled at Jerry's remarks as he uplinked the professional night cameras he'd rented to record the event for fraternity posterity. "This place is perfect. It's scary enough to give Dracula nightmares," he said slamming the trunk lid. "And look at that sky. Those clouds look extremely creepy. It's like a big wave coming at us."

"This terrain reminds me of the *Sleepy Hollow* flick," Harry put in. "Look at those gnarled trees, and the fog is getting thicker. Christ!"

"Do you hear hoof beats?" Jerry said in his scariest voice.

"Do unto others like what was done unto us last year," Ben mused.

"Right on! Only ten times worse if we play our cards right," Sam said gleefully. "It's payback time in the old woods tonight."

"Thank God we didn't do the haunted house routine this year. We've been to the old mental hospital one too many times!" Jerry exclaimed.

Sean extracted the ladder from inside the van and propped it against the wall, and one by one, the frats climbed the wall of the compound and descended to the ground on the other side. The new recruits were to arrive shortly, and five of the six early birds needed to find their places in the bushes to prepare for the insidious pranks they had devised for hell night over the past few weeks. Ben handed the newly painted metal sign they had brought with them down to Walt, who leaned it against a stump adjacent to the entrance where the recruits were certain to see it. The sign was shiny and white with big red letters that read, "BEWARE! This area patrolled by vicious attack dogs!"

Ben snickered as he took his position in the bushes and sat down on the ground to wait for the fun to begin. Sean returned the ladder to the van and drove back to the campus. He had to cram for a test.

The interior of the compound was covered with rough terrain that was perfect for soldiers to play war games; however, Charlie had been told that the five-mile-square training ground was no longer operational since new recruits were being trained at Fort Dix in New Jersey.

A half an hour later, another van pulled up to the main entrance to the compound, and three new recruits and three current members exited the van. Milo extracted a ladder from the luggage rack atop the van and propped it against the ten-foot-tall fence. Justin, another current member, laughed insidiously as the group assembled for instructions.

Mark, the president of Alpha Phi Omega, addressed the blindfolded trio, who were already sweating bullets. "OK, plebes, the way this works is you are to climb this ladder, and lower yourselves down into the compound on the other side of this fence. You are to stay inside until we return to pick you up at seven o'clock tomorrow morning. If for any reason you leave the area before we arrive, you will be immediately disqualified from membership into APO. No matter what you may hear or see during the night, you must hang in there until morning."

"What do you mean by that, Mark?" questioned Marty as he looked about inquisitively.

"Hey, you dumb shit, that's for us to know and for you to find out. Here's a flashlight so you don't kill yourself running into trees. Now get your asses over the fence so we can get on with setting up the frat house for tomorrow's big bash."

The recruits dutifully climbed the ladder and lowered themselves down into the quivering darkness that lay silent behind the wall. The ground was covered in mist, and an eerie breeze whined in the trees.

"Legend has it," Milo piped in, "that some soldiers died a hard death behind these walls during the Civil War, and sometimes they come looking for the ones that tortured them to death."

"You don't believe in ghosts, do you?" Mark laughed, and the other two made spooky noises as they threw the ladder into the back of the van, climbed aboard, and drove off.

When the van's headlights disappeared, the whole area was enveloped in total blackness. There was no moon. Even the stars had disappeared into the dark thunderclouds.

"Christ, it's dark out here. Snap on that flashlight!" the recruit named Robert ordered.

"Who died and made you boss?" Craig retorted, visibly nervous from the pitch-blackness. "Where is your flashlight? Did you leave it in the van?"

"Of course not, numb nuts! We don't want to use up all our batteries in the first hour. We need to conserve," Robert replied.

The light from Craig's flashlight darted about the area where they were standing, but the beam did little to illuminate the dense terrain within.

Suddenly, Marty's eyes fell upon the big red letters of the sign Walt had strategically placed just before their arrival.

"What's this shit? 'BEWARE! This area patrolled by vicious attack dogs!'" Marty whined. "Those guys wouldn't put us in here with a bunch of Dobermans would they?"

"No way! We're just joining a club, not offering up our lives to martyrdom. What good are we to the frat if we're dead?" Robert answered.

Just then the sound of vicious, barking dogs in the distance split the silence.

"This can't be happening; those bastards wouldn't do this to us."

"Hey, guys, take a good look at this sign. It looks like it was just painted. Do you think that somebody's just reactivated these digs for combat, and Mark and the guys don't know about it?" The sound of the dogs got louder from the left and seemed to be getting closer.

"I don't know about you guys, but I'm not staying around here to find out." The threesome ran to the fence and started trying to help each other up to the top. The sound of the dogs was getting uneasily closer. The fence was too high for them to climb, and they finally had to give up trying to scale it.

"Let's find a tree to climb away from the barking. We need to get off the ground," Marty shouted.

They all turned on their flashlights since they couldn't see their hands in front of their faces in the pitch-blackness.

Without warning, the sound of the dogs began directly in front of them. They immediately turned to flee in another direction.

"I can almost feel the gnashing of teeth on my legs," Craig whimpered. "Maybe I'm not Alpha Phi Omega material after all."

"Shut the hell up and find a tree!" Marty screamed.

Like madmen they veered to the center of the woods. They ran and ran in a frantic flight for survival. The lights from the flashlight danced chaotically through the undergrowth. Their faces and arms were bleeding from the limbs that cut into their flesh as they ran blindly into the terrain in search of a tree that would allow them to get off the ground before the dogs found them.

Totally exhausted, Marty grabbed Robert and Craig, and they paused to survey the situation under a large tree they had approached.

Marty looked at the limbs on this tree that were lower than any they had come upon and considered it climbable. "Help me reach that limb, and I'll pull you up."

"Turn off that light," Robert gasped as he tried to catch his breath and lifted Marty higher in order to reach the lowest limb.

"This tree isn't overly substantial, but at least we're off the ground," Craig exclaimed as the three recruits found purchase on their own limb of the tree.

The sound of the dogs ceased abruptly. After a minute of silence, the barking resumed, but now it seemed as if it had moved closer to the entrance than it had been a minute ago. Then as before, it stopped entirely. Five minutes passed, and the barking started again to the left of where they had first heard the hellish sound.

"Shit! It sounds like the whole woods are filled with these fucking hounds!" Craig muttered and bit his fingertips nervously.

"Quiet, we need to think," Marty said.

"We'd better think fast...I don't think we're far enough off the ground to save our asses," Robert whined as he eyed the distance to the ground.

Suddenly, the sound of a vicious dog scared the threesome shitless, piercing their ears as if the dogs had climbed the same tree they were hidden in. They looked at each other and waited for the gnashing teeth.

Marty turned his flashlight toward the limbs behind them. There, taped to a branch, was a big, black speaker pouring out the sound of a pack of vicious, barking dogs.

"Those assholes," Craig shouted with a sigh of relief. "This is all a hoax after all. Boy, they really had us going for a while."

"That's not what you said five minutes ago. Let's hope that they didn't hear you whimpering like a wuss," Robert reminded Craig.

"Quiet!" Marty whispered. "Let's play along with them until morning or when they call us to come out." The sound from the speaker that was piercing their ears stopped abruptly. They waited in silence for ten minutes, which seemed like an hour.

"It appears that our comrades have decided to call it quits. They've turned off the sound system. They must be getting thirsty for a brew," Robert said as they waited for the barking to return.

"Not so fast," cautioned Marty. "I don't think they've doled out enough torture. Last year's plebes were under the gun for five hours, according to what I was told. I'd rather be sitting here in this tree chilling rather than being abused all night. Let's lay low a while longer."

Finally, after another hour passed and there was still no barking, the three recruits climbed down from the tree and started walking back toward the entrance. Their eyes had grown more accustomed to the dark, and they proceeded stealthily without the aid of their flashlights.

Marty, who was leading the threesome, stumbled over something in his path, and he fell forward on top of it. His hand landed on a pile of something wet, warm, and grisly. He jumped up and turned the flashlight on it.

"It looks like Jerry," Marty said as the others turned on their flashlights and shined them on the fallen frat brother, who was lying face down on the path with his eyes closed in what appeared to be a pool of blood. His shirt and jeans were shredded and streaked with dark stains.

"C'mon, Jerry. Get up! We're on to you. We found the speakers. You're going to need a lot more vampire blood to fool us," Robert barked triumphantly.

Jerry lay still. Blood seemed to ooze from several holes in his shirt and from a horrible gash on his thigh.

Craig nudged him with his shoe, but Jerry didn't move and continued to ooze.

"Stop clowning, Jerry. Enough is enough," Marty said as he turned him over and shone the flashlight on his face.

One of Jerry's eyes was dangling from its socket, and his throat has been ripped out. The threesome stood aghast. They couldn't fathom what was happening, but they knew something had gone very wrong. What was supposed to be a big joke was now a big disaster, and their very lives were on the line.

On the ground beside Jerry was a small remote control unit about the size of a TV remote. Marty picked it up and pocketed it.

They stood there in a state of shock, their energy drained. Unexpectedly, the sound of the barking dogs began again. This time much closer than it was before.

"What are we going to do now? It must be a mile to the fence," Craig whimpered. "We'll never make it."

"Let's go back to the tree and think," Robert suggested.

The sound of barking from the direction of the tree dismissed this idea.

Suddenly they heard someone screaming and flailing through the underbrush in the distance, and all at once they saw a figure running into the clearing before them. A pack of large black dogs that appeared to be Dobermans were chomping at the heels of the screaming frat brother. They all recognized the familiar voice of Ben, who was communicating at a higher octave than usual, but his voice was still recognizable.

Harry, another brother, was writhing on the ground about fifty feet to the left of where Ben had come running. He was being eaten alive by another pack of voracious canines.

The threesome hesitated for a moment to decide whether to attempt to rescue one or both of their beloved frat brothers or to make a second attempt at scaling the ten-foot fence and escape with their lives. A violent ripping sound followed by silence answered their question as Harry stopped struggling and let the dogs have their way with him without further interference.

"We've got to get their attention away from us," Robert exclaimed as he remembered Jerry's remote that Marty had picked up. "Turn on the barking with the remote. Maybe it will distract them."

Marty turned on the back left speaker, and the barking started behind them and to the right as they faced the fence. They bolted as the dogs ignored them and continued ripping Ben and Harry's flesh into bloody bits. The recruits ran as fast as their legs would carry them into the woods. They stayed as much away from the branches and underbrush as they could without any light to guide them. The pitiful cries of other frat brothers filled the night in every direction as the sound of barking, both real and staged, filled the compound.

They finally made it to the clearing and the entrance of the compound. Behind the fence, an empty van sat with its headlights on shining toward the fence. The headlights allowed them to see the horror that continued to unfold.

To the right, they saw Mark hanging from a tree limb with five Dobermans trying to sink their teeth into his butt, hell-bent on pulling him to the ground. Mark screamed with each lunge of the vicious attack dogs.

After several futile attempts at reaching him, two of the dogs started jumping up to grab the end of the limb Mark was hanging from with their teeth. This brought the limb closer to the ground and allowed the other dogs to finally reach him.

A scream of mortal pain filled their ears as the weight of three Doberman's hanging by their teeth from his exposed body finally brought Mark to the ground with a sickening thud. The dogs all joined in the feast as his body was tossed to and fro like a puppet as he succumbed to a sea of bloody teeth.

The recruits moved as fast and silently as they could to the left toward the fence. Robert and Craig both put out their hands to create a foothold for Marty and, with all their strength, lifted him toward the top of the fence, just as another set of hungry dogs spotted them.

Marty finally reached the top of the fence with his hands, and with all his might, he pulled his body to the top and straddled the fence with his legs. With one arm holding on, he reached down for his friends.

The dogs were coming. Their eyes blazed with frenzy. Craig grabbed Marty's hand, and Robert lifted him up as high as he could until Craig grabbed the top of the fence with his other hand. Robert jumped desperately to grab onto Craig's body to escape the Doberman onslaught. He couldn't hold on and was immediately covered with the black vicious beasts, which ripped him to shreds.

Craig was also not high enough to escape the wrath of the vicious hounds, and he too was pulled from Marty's arms and devoured by the raging throng. Marty slipped from his perch atop the fence and fell to the ground on the other side. The dogs ran back and forth along the fence trying to find a way to get to him.

Tears streamed down his face that was covered with blood from the ordeal he alone had survived. He lay there wailing, shrieking, and cursing the loss of his friends and the pointlessness of their supreme sacrifice.

As he lifted his eyes from the ground, he realized he had fallen upon a battered sign lying all but buried in the thick grass. He turned it over and lifted it toward the headlights that were still ablaze on the van. The dirty white sign was pocked with bullet holes and still had a big spike hanging from the top where it apparently had been affixed to something. He read the big red letters that would haunt him for the rest of his life, "BEWARE! This area patrolled by vicious attack dogs!!!!"

* * *

SURPRISE! SURPRISE!

Two bodies involved in a head-on collision earlier that week were just delivered to the Morningside Funeral Home. When their Lincoln Town Car collided with a semi carrying steel beams, the young man was decapitated and his fiancé lost the upper right quarter of her face. Both died instantly.

Jane Regan, who was working late, called the owner, Gregory Stickley, to inform him of the delivery.

Gregory, his new wife, Mandy, and her two daughters, Cindy and Sandy, were sitting at a large dining room table when the call came in. A large birthday cake with forty candles had been placed in the middle of the table.

"Can't you call Henry to take care of this tonight?" Mandy said in exasperation. "It's your birthday, and we are so looking forward to the party I planned for you."

"Darling, I know you're disappointed, but we can have the party tomorrow night."

"Day-old cake won't taste the same, I promise you."

"Order a new cake if it makes you happy." Gregory kissed her on the cheek and threw two kisses to Cindy and Sandy as he departed through the door that led to the garage and his Lexus.

When Gregory arrived at the funeral home, Jane was typing correspondence in the office on the first floor.

"When did the accident victims arrive?"

"Larry and Steve wheeled the gurneys into the lab about seven p.m. I called Henry, but couldn't reach him. I think he said he was going to the movies with Blanch. Do you want me to try again?"

"No, there's no need. My fortieth birthday party has been ruined tonight, so I may as well let Henry enjoy the rest of his evening. I can get the ball rolling, and Henry can finish up tomorrow."

Jane looked at Gregory suspiciously, and after weighing his comments concerning Henry, she looked at the calendar on her Rolodex and said, "It really is your birthday...April second...how could I have forgotten?"

"I was about to blow out the candles when you called. Mandy and the kids are really mad at you for breaking up such a lavish affair."

"You really didn't need to be here tonight. Henry could have handled it."

Gregory ignored this comment. "Why are you working overtime?"

"I'm not working overtime," Jane retorted. "I need to take some personal leave, and I was cleaning out my inbox."

"Did you call the temp agency?"

"Of course I did. I wouldn't leave without getting someone to fill in while I'm gone. I would think you would know that by now."

"Hey, I apologize," Gregory said as he paced back and forth across the office and poured himself a cup of stale coffee. "Do what you've got to do, and come back as soon as you can. You know I can't get along without you."

This comment rekindled some old emotions for Jane, at least for a split second, but the reality of recent events restored her deep hatred for Gregory almost as fast.

"Look, I'd better get started." Gregory pitched the remnants of the coffee in the trashcan. "As I've indicated in the past. I don't want to be disturbed once I start the embalming process."

Jane looked at him with a sideways glance and reached for her purse from under her desk. She started to straighten a few sticky notes in her daybook as Gregory opened the door that led to the basement. She heard the bolt click before he descended the stairs.

Jane extracted a sealed letter of resignation from her purse and placed it in the middle of her desk. She took one last look around the office and left the building for the last time.

She got into her car and drove to a local restaurant. She requested a quiet table, and the maître d' escorted her to a table toward the back. She pulled her cell phone from her purse and dialed Mandy.

"Oh, hello, Mandy. This is Jane at Morningside. Gregory told me he's feeling really guilty about not celebrating his birthday with you and the kids. After all, forty is a milestone, and it should be special. I suggest you and the kids come over to the office. We can have a surprise party for Gregory here. I don't know if you know this, but Gregory loves surprises."

"Really? The kids will be so excited."

"I left the back door to the basement open for you. I'll be helping Gregory with paperwork, and Henry will be processing the bodies. Just come on in with the cake, and we'll all yell 'surprise' as soon as we see you."

"You don't know how much this means to the kids and me, Jane. Let's have lunch sometime this week. I'd like to get to know you a little better."

"You don't need to thank me. Seeing the look on Gregory's face will be reward enough for me. Don't wait too long before you come. I'm really looking forward to the party."

Jane returned her cell to her purse and started perusing the menu. She thought a very dry martini would be the perfect drink to celebrate Gregory's birthday.

Mandy pulled around back of the funeral home, as Jane had suggested, and parked the Mercedes next to one of the black hearses. The only lights that were on in the building were in the basement. There was a low drone of rock music throbbing from within.

Mandy shushed the kids and told them to be very quiet, as to not spoil the surprise. She placed the cake on a table on the porch and quickly lit the candles. Cindy and Sally giggled excitedly as Mandy opened the door.

They burst into the lab and screamed merrily, "Surprise! Surprise!"

The threesome was blinded momentarily by the bright fluorescent lights and disoriented by an earsplitting sound of Sam the Sham's great rock classic, "Wooly Bully."

When their eyes adjusted to the lights, Mandy and the kids stood frozen in a state of shock at the sight they would remember until the day they died. Gregory was nude atop the naked female corpse on the embalming table. His hands were squeezing her large breasts in unison with each violent thrust of his hips. His eyes were closed tight in a fit of ecstasy, unaware that Mandy and the kids had entered the room.

The right quarter of the young woman's face was a hollow cavern of gore and the absence of her right cheek gave her exposed teeth a sardonic smile.

Mandy fled with the kids and called the police. The two officers who answered the call also found Gregory in a fit of ecstasy with his eyes closed until they cuffed him.

Gregory committed suicide in the fifth year of his ten-year prison sentence for necrophilia due to a severe case of hemorrhoids.

* * *

RAVENOUS

After a week of feeling poorly, I made an appointment with a doctor. A week later, I went to the doctor's office, signed in, and took a seat in the waiting room.

I was getting weaker each day and I was very worried that so many strange symptoms had cropped up so quickly. I was beginning to look like an albino. My skin was very pale, and my eyes were bloodshot.

The nurse called "Charles Simmons," and I followed her into a room to wait for the doctor.

We made small talk as she weighed me, checked my blood pressure, and took my temperature. She looked at the results quizzically and checked my blood pressure and temperature a second time.

"Is something wrong?" I asked.

"Your blood pressure and your temperature are unusually low."

"What does it mean?"

"Don't be alarmed. The doctor will be in shortly and discuss the findings with you."

She scurried out of the room before I could muster another question. I tried to feel my blood pressure by pressing on the artery in my neck, but I couldn't feel anything. It did feel uncommonly chilly in the room. I saw goose bumps rise on my arm and shivered.

I heard a knock, and Dr. Frank entered the room and took a seat. After reviewing my chart, he checked my blood pressure and my temperature for the third time, which I found peculiar.

"How do you feel, Charles?" he asked as he reviewed my chart.

"I feel ravenous, but I can't keep anything down. I am very weak."

"Have you ever had an iron deficiency?"

"Not that I know of."

Looking at the chart, the doctor asked, "You say you don't have diabetes?"

"Not that I know of."

"You aren't taking any kind of medication?"

"No."

"You're not allergic to anything?"

"I filled out all this information on your questionnaire," I said wearily.

"Bear with me," the doctor replied, picking up his stethoscope. "I'm just verifying a few things pertinent to diagnosing your problem."

He had me lie down on the examination table and asked me to remove my shirt.

He started moving the freezing metal chest piece across my bare skin and began listening. He asked me to take some deep breaths and continued with his questions.

"Have you visited any foreign countries in the last year?"

"Yes. My friends and I did a European tour about six months ago."

He beckoned me to sit up and said, "You can put your shirt on." Making a note in the chart, he continued, "When did you begin to feel weak?"

"I'd say about the middle of March."

"This is September...so that would put it not long after your trip."

"I guess so. I never had any reason to suspect the trip had anything to do with my problem."

"Did you visit any of the Baltic countries?"

"We did. We toured Finland, Germany, Russia, Sweden, and even stayed in a castle in Transylvania, which was in Romania."

"During your travels, did you eat anything that disagreed with you?"

"Not that I recall."

"When you were on vacation, did anything happen to you that was out of the ordinary?"

"If you count getting bitten by a bat out of the ordinary, I guess it did. We were sitting around a campfire at what was called the 'Count's Castle' having some brews and shooting the shit, when this big winged thing swooped down and took a piece out of my neck."

The doctor pulled back my shirt collar and looked at my neck. He surveyed the tiny scar atop the jugular vein and said, "The wound is aggravated and red. I'll give you a prescription for some salve to put on it."

"We talked about the bat for months. It was so eerie to be bitten by a bat in a castle in Transylvania, but it turned out to be nothing. I went to a local hospital, and they tested me for rabies to be sure. I got a clean bill of health."

The doctor looked at me with concern and said, "Charles, I am going to try to get you admitted today at St. Barnabus. We need to do quite a few tests, and I think time is of the essence."

"What do you think it is? Is it life threatening?"

"I hate to alarm you, but as your doctor, I have to be frank. You don't have a pulse, and I've examined corpses that had a higher temperature than you have. Your vitals are telling me you are already dead, but since you are talking to me, there must be some other explanation."

"Dead? There must be something wrong with your equipment. I must have some kind of stomach virus that's preventing me to keep down solid foods. If I could get some nourishment, I'd be fine."

"An ambulance will arrive within the hour to take you to the hospital."

"Do you think the bat has something to do with this?"

"I do," the doctor said as he stood and withdrew toward the door. "Judging from the way you look, your ravenous hunger, your lack of blood pressure and body heat, if vampires were real, I would say that you are in the early stages of becoming one."

"That's absurd. Vampires only exist in folklore."

"I have never had a patient like you before, but I have read about people who believe they have become vampires, and once they have tasted human blood, they can no longer tolerate eating normal food. Since you can no longer eat food and you have become deathly pale, you may soon require an infusion of blood to stay alive or to remain in whatever state you're in now."

I looked at the doctor like he had two heads and recalled how my incisors had been aching the past few weeks. Everything he was saying, no matter how bizarre, seemed to explain my current condition.

"Over the last few weeks, have you experienced any inclination to attack a human?"

"Of course not. I could never harm another person. You must be some kind of nutcase."

I arose from my chair to leave when a strange sensation swept over me.

Suddenly the thought of human blood gripped me with an uncontrollable desire to sink my teeth into the doctor's jugular. The doctor's bulging eyes told me he was feeling a menacing apprehension in my attitude as he put down my chart on the table and moved toward the door.

I felt my teeth reshaping into the fangs of a vampire as the doctor stared at me in a grip of horror.

In the blink of an eye, I swooped upon him and began to quench my insatiable hunger with his warm, delicious blood. I called for the nurse, and then the receptionist, and also ravaged one occupant remaining in an examination room. The office had closed for the day, and there were no more patients outside in the waiting room to call in.

I was feeling much better, but I still had room for the ambulance drivers.

* * *

TOMORROW IS A LONG TIME

She awoke in a cold sweat. The whisper of a scream seemed to linger in her subconscious. Fear had been her sleeping partner this night, but the nightmare had subsided and she couldn't remember any part of it.

Her eyes fell upon a pink stain on the carpet she had never seen before. There was an eerie silence that hung heavy in the room. She began to tremble and her heart started beating rapidly as her eyes darted from one side of the bedroom to the other, but after a thorough inspection, everything seemed to be in its place.

Not only was everything in its place, her room was as neat as a pin. Someone had picked up the clutter that was strewn about the room when she had gone to bed. She had never seen her room in this condition. She even thought she detected a lingering smell of furniture polish in the air. How strange for her mother to tidy up her room while she had been asleep. Was it her birthday? Had she done something special to deserve this unexpected surprise?

The bedroom seemed very stuffy, and the glare from the window seemed unnaturally bright for this time of the morning. Time. The word stuck in her mind as she looked to the nightstand for her clock. Incredibly, it was ten after twelve.

What was the matter? She had never overslept this long before. Nothing made any sense. She jumped out of bed and dressed as quickly as she could. She needed answers. There were too many mysteries for one morning.

She assumed that everyone was waiting in the living room to spring the surprise on her. Everyone knew what was happening but her. As she was leaving her room, she saw a card lying on the bureau. It was crumpled and seemed wet to the touch. She opened it and read the words aloud to the silent room: "We offer our sincerest condolences in your time of grief. Signed John and Martha Jonas."

She darted into the living room with expectation, "Mom! Dad! I saw a card on the bureau, and it says someone has died!"

To her surprise, there was no one there. She heard the sound of a car starting up outside in the driveway. She ran to the front door, opened it, and peered out. Her mother and father were pulling out of the driveway. Both were dressed as if they were going to church. She yelled to get their attention, but they didn't hear her. They continued into the street and pulled away. She jumped the steps on the front porch and ran into the street screaming at the top of her lungs, but the green sedan never paused.

She sat down on a bench in front of her neighbors' house and began to sob. Everything was creepy, and the memory of a terrible nightmare she couldn't remember lingered in her subconscious. She noticed several people walking across the street who went about their business without wondering why she was crying.

She returned home and found a rose petal on the sidewalk that led to the front door. She gripped it tightly and tried to make sense of it all: The card. The roses. Her tidy room. Her mother dressed in black.

Everything pointed to a funeral. But for whom? Why hadn't she been told someone had died, and why was she left out when they went to the wake? She was certainly old enough to attend. It didn't make any sense.

She wiped her tears on her sleeve and proceeded to the next-door neighbors' house to ask if they knew who had died, but they, too, were not at home.

She left their house and started walking. Block after block she pondered the circumstances without resolve. The people passing were faceless; the shop windows downtown passed in a flurry. The world was just the patterns of the sidewalk.

But then a familiar object restored her train of thought. She saw her parents' car parked on the street in front of her. She saw "Springdale Funeral Home" on a sign to the left. She remembered she had been here before when Aunt Rose died. She paused for a moment and went in.

The air of sorrow and mourning sucked her breath away in an instant. It was like she had entered another world. She heard people weeping somewhere within, and an organ was playing music that was so melancholy, it brought tears to her eyes. The interior was dark, and candles were flickering in each shadowed room along the corridor. She heard a minister praying, but couldn't understand the words.

Step by step, she inched forward. The fragrance of many kinds of flowers bombarded her senses and made her feel queasy. She entered a dark room where shadowy people bowed and prayed and sat sobbing around a circle of chairs. She faced the party of mourners and seemed to recognize almost everyone.

With every step toward the casket, the nightmare she couldn't remember returned with a vengeance. She was at her sweet-sixteen birthday party. She was so happy until the party was over. Afterward, the images returned in a flurry of terror. The man. The window. The knife. The scream. The blood. It all seemed so real, and she remembered every detail.

"No!" she screamed as the tears rolled down her face. "It wasn't a dream! It was real!"

The casket came into view, and her eyes fell across her own face lying within. Turning away from the horror she had tried so desperately to forget, she saw her mother weeping in a pew a few yards away.

She had been cheated. She was never going to college. She was never going to be married and have children like all the girls she had invited to the sweet-sixteen party. She didn't want to go into the light that beckoned to her now. She wanted so much to hold on to life a little while longer and stay with the ones who loved her. But when she looked into her mother's eyes, there was nothing left to hold on to. They were the eyes of someone who had lost her little girl.

* * *

THE AX

Orville and Pam Miller left Town and Country Realty excited and smiling from ear to ear. They had just signed the papers on the purchase of their new farm. They joined their two sons, Tim and Bobby, twelve and fourteen, who were waiting with the windows down in their old Dodge station wagon. It was a warm summer day in Ipswich, Massachusetts.

"I can't believe we got such a large tract of land for such a low price!" Pam exclaimed.

"I don't get it either," Orville agreed. "It even has a stream running through the property. I think the Joneses were just too old to work it, and a property this big demands a lot of attention."

"We have Tim and Bobby to help us, which gives us an edge. Right, fellas?"

"Right!" the boys answered in harmony and rolled their eyes.

The Millers couldn't wait to get to their new home and start what they hoped would be a wonderful, new life in which they would prosper like they never had before.

That afternoon, the movers arrived and carried their meager belongings into their new home. The next day, they wasted no time beginning to till the land and plant seeds for the autumn harvest. Orville worked harder than he ever had, and even though the effort of running irrigation hookups from the nearby stream was backbreaking, he completed the task with a fury.

On the second week of tilling, Orville uncovered an ax that was buried just below the topsoil level not far from the farmhouse. He picked it up and inspected the blade, which was incredibly sharp. Although it appeared very old, the ax was in remarkable condition for being buried in the ground. Orville saw writing engraved on the back of the blade, but it was too worn to read. He placed the ax in a temporary outbuilding and resumed his daily chores.

After several months of unsuccessful planting, Orville decided to build the barn on the site where the ax was found since nothing they planted would grow there. He enlisted the help of several neighbors on the project in exchange for assisting them when they needed a hand with their crops.

After the first day's hard work was over, Orville and his neighbors sat on the porch to have a beer and shoot the bull before supper.

After a long pull, Brad Peavy, a crusty, old codger who reminded Orville of Slim Pickens, drawled as he soothed his sunburned back with a cold, wet handkerchief: "Orville, I hope you did the right thing buying this place. It sure looks like a good piece of land for farming, but something's not right. There's a funny smell in the air, and it ain't manure. Old Mr. Jones sat right on this very front porch and told me time and again over many a bottle of Bud that nothing would grow in this spot no matter how many times he planted." He picked up a handful of topsoil and let it spill through his fingers.

Jed Flanders, another neighbor who came to help on the project, slapped his neck where a fly had just landed. "And where do these damned horseflies come from? I'm just across the holler, and they're not over there pestering me."

Orville paused for a time, and after making sure Tim and Bobby were out of earshot, he grimaced and said, "I wish I had talked to all of you before I bought this property, but, hey, it's water over the dam now. I'm beginning to have some luck with corn on the North Fork, and this spot where nothing will grow, no matter the reason, is a perfect place for the barn. I'm looking into a bug wacker, maybe two, to take care of the flies." He bowed slightly and began to whisper, "Don't speak too loud when Pam and the boys are around; they get spooked when they hear the stories the city folk tell about this place at the laundromat and at school. Bobby has been having bad dreams almost every night. Pam keeps hearing strange noises in the walls, but each time I look for a varmint, I can't find any."

Leroy Miller, a neighbor with a patch over one eye, pointed toward the ax hanging from some nails on the A-frame. "And what about that ax? Have you ever seen a blade that sharp on an ax? I haven't. Hell. I'll go you one better. I've never seen a machine that could make an ax that sharp."

"Come on, fellas! Cut me some slack. I found the ax buried in the field. Maybe it belonged to Ponce de Leon or one of those Italian explorers. Maybe I found Excalibur in a cow pile. It leaves me alone, and I leave it alone. Maybe it will come in handy when I clear the woods at Possum Point." Orville trailed off, hoping to change the subject.

They all chuckled at Orville's response, but the mystery still lingered in all their minds. Each new day increased their uneasiness.

In another week, the barn was finished, and Orville's neighbors were glad to stop working on his property. The bad smell had gotten progressively worse. Orville had tried several remedies he found at the garden shop that were supposed to combat bad odors; consequently, the pungent smell of mothballs began to hide, or at least diminish, the horrible dead smell that lingered about the property.

Several days later, Orville saw the ax embedded in a stump next to the barn. He called for the boys, who were busy doing their chores nearby, and they came running.

"Who knows why the ax is down from its place in the barn?" Orville questioned.

"I took it down when I noticed the inscription on the blade had changed," Tim explained like he had been caught with his hand in the cookie jar. "I wanted to show it to you, but I got sidetracked when I had to milk the cows. I left it on the stump."

"That's OK, Son. I just wondered why it was there. The blade is so sharp. I'm afraid for you to use it."

"Don't worry, Dad. I don't care if I ever touch it again. I wish we would get rid of the scary thing. I just wondered if you saw how the inscription has changed," Tim explained.

"What do you mean the inscription has changed?" Bobby said as he looked toward the ax in the stump.

"You can read the inscription now. And the blade is getting shinier and, believe it or not, sharper. You don't have to slide your finger down the blade for it to cut you. It will cut you if you lay your finger on the blade. It's that sharp."

"You must be having another bad dream, Son. What you are saying is impossible."

"Take a look for yourself if you don't believe me."

Orville made a beeline to the ax and extracted it effortlessly from the oak stump. He turned it over and looked at it like he had never seen it before. Etched into the blade was the date, October 31, 1697. He couldn't look at it in the bright sunlight; the brilliance hurt his eyes. It was flawless. He stood and removed a handkerchief from his back pocket and let it freefall across the blade. Soundlessly, it separated into two pieces that each floated to the surface of the stump.

They stared at each other in disbelief at what they had seen, but no one said a word. The cool breath of autumn raised the hairs on Orville's neck. Finally, he placed the ax back where it had been mounted in the barn.

The three of them rushed into the farmhouse to tell Pam about the strange metamorphosis that had taken place with the ax. Not finding her in the kitchen, they moved to the living room. Pam sat in a daze with a large sewing needle protruding from her finger. Blood had covered the knee of the blue jeans she was mending and had dripped down, making a large wet stain on the rug.

Orville gasped, and the boys ran screaming to her side. Her eyes were open and staring into space. Orville shook her, and she began to come around. Seeing the blood all over the blue jeans and the rug, she began to scream uncontrollably. Orville spent the next half hour trying to settle her down and find out what had happened.

Pam had no memory of sticking the needle in her finger and couldn't explain why she felt no pain. Later that evening, everything had returned to normal, and the four of them sat in silence at the dinner table thinking about the needle, the blood, and the ax.

"Orville," Pam began, "I know you had your heart set on this place, but something is not right here. I fear if we stay, something bad is going to happen."

"What are you talking about?" Orville countered. "I admit there have been some strange things going on, but nothing bad has happened to any of us until you fell asleep and stuck yourself with that needle."

"Orville Miller," Pam fumed, "don't sit there and tell me I stuck myself with that needle and didn't feel it. You know better than that. It was like I was hypnotized, not asleep."

"Dad," Bobby piped in, "can't you see something bad is living here with us? Can't you feel it? How do you explain the date on the ax? Every day the date gets clearer and the blade gets sharper."

"I believe the ax is an omen," Pam said. "It's telling us that something bad is going to happen on Halloween, which is only ten days away. The date on the ax is October 31, 1697. Is it a coincidence that this Halloween will be three hundred years after that date? Orville, I don't want any of us to be here on that day. Let's visit my mother for a few days until Halloween is over."

"Pam, I can't explain the things that have happened, but you must face the facts, nothing bad has happened to any of us or the livestock. I can't just pick up and leave the animals without food and water, and I can't ask the neighbors to take care of them for no reason."

Pam shook her head and left the room crying. The boys looked at each other in disbelief that their father still didn't want to leave even after their mother's unexplained trance and the frightening episode with the ax.

As each day passed and Halloween grew nearer, the barn began to smell as if all the horses that were housed there had died and their flesh was rotting in their stalls. The horseflies were even bigger and more aggressive than before as they swarmed over everything. They were buzzing like bees on every windowpane. Each time Tim and Bobby made a trip to the barn, they had to cover themselves from head to toe with burlap to protect them from the unforgiving onslaught of flies. On October 26, they found the horses and chickens dead in pools of maggots on the barn floor. The stench was unbearable.

The loss of the livestock had finally pushed Orville over the edge. It was time to get his family out of there, at least until after Halloween. They hurriedly packed a bag and left everything they had saved for all their lives and departed in the Dodge station wagon. A swarm of big black horseflies covered the car windows as Orville sped away from the farmhouse down the gravel road that led to Ipswich.

The Millers arrived in Ipswich, which was truly a refreshing change. They decided to go to the mall in hopes they could find something other than the farm to think about for a time. This world was bright and cheerful. People were laughing and talking. Everything seemed normal once again.

"Orville," Pam said as the four of them huddled around a table in the food court, "let's cut our losses and forget the farm. We can move in with my dad until we can get our feet back on the ground."

"You're forgetting one thing: Everything we have is tied up in the farm, and the bank is going to foreclose if we don't pay the mortgage. We'll never be able to sell the farm to anyone in the state it's in. We'll be bankrupt, and our credit will be shot for years."

"I'd rather be bankrupt than dead. Something bad is going to happen, and I don't want to be there when it does. The children aren't safe there, and you know it." Pam started to cry.

"Dad, please don't make us go back. We're afraid. Our animals are dead, and what killed them will surely kill us if we go back," Bobby wailed.

"You don't have to go back," Orville said. "I wouldn't do anything to put any of you in harm's way."

Orville put his arms around Pam and the kids to comfort them as the thought of losing everything weighed heavily on his mind.

"Don't cry, honey. I need to think this thing over. Let's go to Herb's place. Maybe we'll come up with something."

The boys were silent, but relieved that returning to the farm was on hold for the time being.

After consoling Pam and the kids for a time, they returned to the station wagon and headed for Pam's father's house on the other side of town.

Later that evening, Orville had a beer with Herb, Pam's father, on the back porch. Pam and the boys were inside watching TV.

"I've never heard of anything like this in all my days. It sounds like something out of the Bible, like a prophecy of some kind. There's been so much strange stuff lately—hurricanes, earthquakes, tornados, mysterious plane crashes, ships disappearing. I heard a couple of meteors just missed us in the last few months, and all the astronomers with all their fancy telescopes didn't know the meteors were out there until they were past us for three or four days."

"Well, Herb, it sounds like the man upstairs didn't think it was time to call in his markers. Think of all the soothsayers that have been predicting the end of the world since time began. Each time the day comes they have predicted and nothing happens, they change to another day. I understand that millions of books have been sold to people who like to read about how close we are to obliteration."

"I've got one of those books in my bookcase right now—*Kiss Your Ass Goodbye*."

"You wasted your money on that gibberish."

"Maybe so, but it was something to pass the time."

"Did you feel better after you read it?"

"Maybe not better, but it did hold my interest."

"Did the author set a date for Armageddon?"

"I don't think he had a specific day. He just said the signs were pointing to someday soon."

"He was a smart man. He didn't give himself a way to make a total fool of himself."

"Well, how do you explain what's happening at the farm?"

"I can't explain it. But I'm not going to give up on all I've worked for without a fight."

"How are you gonna fight something you can't see?"

"All I know is something happened October 31, 1697, and from all indications, it's going to happen again this Friday. I need to do some research on the matter. Maybe the library is a place to start."

"For a man who doesn't believe in Armageddon, it sounds like you're becoming a believer."

"Hey, I didn't say I didn't believe in the devil."

He finished the last swallow of beer and went to bed.

The next morning, bright and early, Orville left Pam and the kids with Herb and drove into Ipswich. He arrived just as the library was opening at 9:00 a.m.

He queried the computer database about the history of the town in every way he could think of, but his unfamiliarity with the library filing system made research difficult. He was getting nowhere after struggling for almost two hours.

He went to the desk where the staff was checking in books and asked if they could recommend an approach to finding out what happened in the Ipswich area in 1697.

A thin elderly lady with a little too much makeup and too long a hairdo for her age suggested speaking with Professor Gardner, who taught history at the high school until he retired. She pointed to a bespectacled elderly man with snow-white hair who was browsing through the magazine rack.

Orville thanked the lady and approached Gardner, who gave him a pleasant smile and adjusted his glasses as Orville started to speak, "Professor Gardner, the lady at the desk said you might be able to help me. Do you have a moment?"

"Son, I hope I have more than a moment, but at my age you never know." He smiled warmly as he dispensed the magazines and took a chair at the closest table.

Orville sat down next to him and gathered his thoughts a bit before speaking. "Professor Gardner..."

"Feel free to call me Hank."

"Hank," said Orville, "I desperately need to find out what happened in these parts in 1697. Could you suggest what book I should look at or someone I can talk to that can shed some light on something that long ago."

"Do you mean the Ipswich area specifically?" The old man scratched his head and looked at Orville with warm curiosity.

"I bought a farm in what they call the North Fork area of Ipswich, and I found an ax buried in the ground when we were tilling that has the date October 31, 1697, etched into the blade." Orville paused, thinking how insane what he was about to say would sound, then continued, "It's a long story, too fantastic for me to even tell you without you thinking I've lost my marbles, but—"

"Slow down, Son. Take it easy. I think you've come to the right person, if I do say so myself. I might be the only one around this town who can help you. The only thing of historical note that occurred around here that year was the execution of an alleged warlock who placed a curse on all the ancestors who were present when he was burned at the stake."

"You know about it?"

"Well, Son, when you teach history for forty years, you kind of get interested in finding out the history of where you live just in case someone asks.. When I started teaching, I researched the history of this town as far back as when William Henry founded it in 1632. Not much that would tickle anyone's fancy occurred until the witch trials started in the eighties. I'll bet you didn't know that seventeen women were tortured and executed as witches right where the town square stands today. Innocent people were accused, prosecuted, and condemned to torture and death at the whim of the magistrates who were in power at the time. Mostly women who didn't suit the masses for whatever reason were singled out and accused of consorting with the devil. After we tortured the poor souls until they confessed to things they'd never done, we hanged them or burned them in a public execution for every man, woman, and child to see."

"That is interesting, but you mentioned a warlock. Is that like the boogeyman? A troll? It's just a character in folklore, isn't it?"

"A warlock is a male version of the witch. It was an evil man who consorted with the devil. He sold his soul in exchange for the promise of eternal life or illimitable dominion over mankind. Keep in mind that vampires, werewolves, and all kinds of monsters were taken much more seriously in the old days than today. Most people were extremely superstitious and lived their life in fear of things that go bump in the night."

"But there's no such thing as vampires and werewolves."

"That's my opinion."

"Was even one woman killed for witchcraft that anyone proved was really a witch?"

"There were plenty of so-called eyewitness accounts of witchcraft and consorting with the devil, but after the lawmakers finally required hard evidence to substantiate unfounded accusations, the last witch was set free. That was three hundred years ago."

"I find it hard to believe that such things exist. That's what makes what's happening on my farm so bizarre. It can't be happening, but it is."

"Did any farm animals die?"

"How did you know?"

"Was there a swarm of flies? A bad smell?" Hank questioned.

"How did you know?" Orville looked at Gardner like he had just seen a ghost. "Are you a mind reader?"

"No, but in my research of the event, I remember the same thing happened for several months after the warlock was burned at the stake. The story is this warlock, whose name was Eli Enoch, may have been the granddaddy of all serial killers in this country. He supposedly murdered hundreds of families with his magic ax in this region over a ten-year period. The killings were the most brutal ever recorded in those days. The victims' body parts were hung from hooks suspended from the ceiling of their homes. A group of townspeople were dedicated to tracking him down before he devoured everyone. They hunted him relentlessly with the help of some of the Native American tribes for years without success. They came upon him several times while he was in the midst of his human feast, but they were unable to subdue him because of his superhuman strength and abilities that were greater than a mortal man. Many of his pursuers became new victims for his atrocities."

Orville raised his hand in front of Hank's face as if he were stopping traffic and remarked, "Hank, if this warlock was so damned superhuman, how did they capture him? Why did he let himself be burned at the stake? Did they sprinkle a little kryptonite on him?"

"On the day you mentioned, a band of trackers came upon Eli after he had devoured a family of eight and had gorged himself to such an extent that he had fallen asleep. His bulging stomach was so enlarged that it appeared ready to burst. A cauldron of blood from the victims was boiling and a mysterious book was open to the bloody notations of a ritual he was trying to complete when they came upon him. He probably would never have been captured if not for the deep stupor that allowed his enemies to finally subdue him."

Orville pondered a moment and said, "Reminds me of what Arnold said about the monster in *Predator*: 'If it bleeds we can kill it.'"

Hank scratched his head and slowly lifted himself from his chair.

"Relax a minute," Hank said with an arthritic wince. "I want to read you a section from my book that was documented as an eyewitness account of the execution." Hank disappeared behind the rows of books for a few moments and reappeared with a one that appeared very old, yet still had the cover intact and the pages tightly bound. It was titled *The Warlock of Ipswich*, and the author was, in fact, Henry Gardner.

"I guess I really did come to the right place to find out what happened in 1697."

Hank smiled proudly and thumbed through the pages until pausing at a section about twenty pages from the back cover.

He hesitated, reading a few passages under his breath, and then started reading aloud in a library whisper.

"'The band of townspeople fell upon him and battered his skull in with their clubs. They bound him with heavy ropes, and while he was unconscious, they cut off his hands and feet. Without a shred of remorse, they blinded him with a poker from the fireplace. At last, assuming he was finally powerless to harm them, they carted him off to a place that had been used as a gallows and once to burn a witch at the stake.'"

"They made Eli a quadriplegic! I guess that did slow him down a little," Orville chirped.

Hank paused and looked at Orville over the top of his eyeglasses, and his voice increased slightly in volume, "Here's the part I believe will be the most interesting to you." Hank continued reading from the book. "'They hoisted him on the gallows and suspended him over a bonfire they had prepared for the occasion. It was almost midnight when all the citizens of the town assembled for the execution. Clergymen began to pray in unison in a ceremony that must have been in those times a kind of exorcism. After the completion of the religious rite, they set the wood on fire and continued to pray as the horrible warlock went up in flames. They tried to destroy the ax, but after their efforts were unsuccessful, they threw it into the flames.'"

A bead of sweat began to run down Orville's face as a heavy rain pelted the library windows in front of them.

Hank continued, "'Suddenly an inhuman scream came from the fire, and a deep voice filled the night as if amplified by the devil. The warlock's hands and feet reappeared from their stubs, and two fierce eyes protruded from his black empty sockets.'" Hank turned the page and went on. "'The demon's words pierced the ears of the crowd with a force that was excruciating and almost maddening.'"

"That's some story," Orville muttered.

Hank looked up for a moment and continued. "I don't know how accurate this is, but this is what an eyewitness wrote that Eli said to the crowd. Of course, this was written down the next day, and it might not be verbatim."

"Don't sweat the small stuff," Orville replied anxiously. "Read on."

One of the patrons looked over at them with a look of disgust and moved farther away to a more secluded spot.

Hank's voice took on a more Shakespearian flair as if he were beginning a soliloquy, and the words seemed like a prophesy from the devil. "'Take heed puny mortals,' Hank exclaimed. "'How dare you interfere with my destiny to rule the world and to serve my eternal master, the king of all evil. I have failed him because of you, and on this night, I must pay the ultimate price. But on this day, three hundred years from the stroke of midnight, I will return to finish what I started. My pain is your curse for when I return, all of the ancestors of those who are here tonight will fall to my ax. And I will savor every morsel of their flesh and every drop of their blood.'"

Hank came down from his high horse and continued in a whisper. "'The ax leapt from the flames into his mighty right hand, and he threw it like a bolt of lightning from his fingertips. The shimmering steel sparkled in the firestorm and swirled like a huge boomerang through the air. The razor-sharp blade swished through the necks of the three clergymen who stood before the warlock and magically returned to his outstretched hand as his body disappeared into the raging inferno. The clergymen's heads fell to the ground, and blood spurted in a scarlet stream from their necks as the crowd began to scream with unbridled horror.'"

"Wow! That's quite a story," Orville mused and scratched his brow. "John Carpenter and Wes Craven must be asleep at the wheel not to have put this warlock on the screen."

Hank looked at him soberly and appeared not to see the levity in Orville's remark. Frowning noticeably, his voice became a bit shaky when he said, "There's one more part I want to share with you before you split your sides laughing."

"Hey, don't be so sensitive," Orville said apologetically. "I just find the whole account something like a story about werewolves and vampires."

"'Despite the fantastic nature of the event, there were over two hundred eyewitnesses to the execution of the warlock and the death of the three clergymen. In researching my book, I found over fifty accounts from those at the scene that were written by what we might call the reporters of the day. Every account is identical. Unlike the crucifixion of Christ, the accounts were written within days of the actual event. The graves of the three clergymen are in the Old Wakefield Cemetery.'"

"You're not saying you believe the warlock was real and was really consorting with the devil? I thought you didn't believe in werewolves and vampires and such."

"I don't believe in werewolves and vampires, but no one has ever said they were more than folklore. There's never been an eyewitness account of murder at the hands of a werewolf or a vampire. In the case of Eli Enoch, over two hundred people say they saw him kill the three clergymen. How do you explain that?"

Orville's levity softened, and he suddenly realized this was not a fairy tale to Henry Gardner. The two men looked at each other for a moment as if just beginning a game of chess.

"Before you go back to whatever you were doing, I want to show you a few more sections in…my book of fairy tales."

"Hey, man, take it easy. I didn't mean to hurt your feelings. I need your help."

"I want to show you a map I put in my book from a news clipping I found in my research from the *Ipswich Times*."

Hank moved the book to the middle of the table and pointed to a section of the map: "Here, running down the left side of the property, is North River. To the right, about two hundred yards east, is what was called Willow Lake. Do these two landmarks have anything to do with your property?"

Orville stared in amazement at the map of the area surrounding the warlock's execution and said, "This is too spooky to believe. This is exactly the way the boundaries are today. When was this map drawn?"

"A few days after the execution in 1697."

"Well, I was looking for some answers when I came to the library, but I never dreamed it would lead to this." Orville looked at the dark, foreboding sky through the large plate-glass window in front of him.

"Let me show you one more thing." Hank took the book and turned a few pages to a list of names. "This is the reason I decided to write the book. Take a look at the names of all those who attended the execution that fateful night in October 1697."

Orville looked down the page and saw many names he recognized, and suddenly he saw an entry that sent a shiver up his spine. Sherman and Mildred Hinkle. Orville looked up at Hank with his mouth agape and stared in disbelief at the page. His wife had traced her ancestors back to when her family came to America, and Sherman and Mildred Hinkle were the first entries on her family tree.

"What's wrong, Son? You look like you've seen a ghost." The old man looked puzzled.

"I think I did just see a ghost. These two people are the great-great-great-grandfather and grandmother of my wife, Pam."

"Are you sure?"

"I can't be sure, but the two names are the same as on her family tree at home."

"Good God in Heaven. Then that would mean…"

"That if this is not a fairy tale, my wife and children are going to die a horrible death four days from now at the hands of the warlock."

"I believe since you married her you won't be excluded."

"I need to get Pam and the kids and get as far away from here as I can."

"I thought you didn't believe in warlocks?" Hank interjected.

Orville scratched his head and looked into the trees out the library window. After a long silence, he said, "I don't know what I believe, but better safe than sorry."

"I don't know if running away will stop the warlock if he has the powers he professes to have."

"Tell me Professor…Hank, that is. What is your final assessment of the story? What do you think? Is it fact or fiction?"

"I didn't tell you before, but my ancestors also attended the execution. Since I have a big stake in the authenticity, I pulled some strings some years ago with some of my old friends at the police department and had the bodies of the clergymen exhumed. They sent whatever bones were left to the morgue to determine the cause of death. All three had their throats cut by a very sharp blade that severed their heads all the way through. Their heads were separated from each body in the casket."

"It appears that if the warlock returns, we're all going to die at midnight on Halloween night."

"Can your friends on the police force help protect us?"

"My friends are all retired, and the new ones wrote me off as a lunatic."

"Did you try to find any of the others on the list?"

"I told the story to a dozen people, and they all laughed in my face. Most people today don't have a clue about their family tree and don't care about their roots."

"I know you've tried without success," Orville said, "but I have to give it one more try to convince a few of these families that a lot of people are going die if we don't do something to stop the warlock. Do you have a list of the people I could go to who live nearby?"

Hank shook his head and said like he was looking at a man on death row, "Son, I know these people a lot better than you do. Even students I taught in school that had a high regard for me wouldn't listen to a word I said. Most of them thought I had lost my mind. The others humored me for a while, but never intended to get involved. Imagine standing in Times Square in New York City trying to tell the masses that a warlock is coming this Halloween. Don't you see how ridiculous that sounds?"

"My family's lives depend on stopping Eli when he returns. I've got to find a way to convince these people to help me save themselves and…the world."

Hank looked at Orville solemnly and handed him the book. "Good luck, Son. You're going to need it."

"What are you going to do?" Orville asked.

"If Eli comes, and I'm confident he will, I'll be waiting at my house with a gun." Orville looked at him, not understanding. "Not for him. For me," Hank said as he stared into the rain. "Maybe you should think about this yourself. It won't be pretty if he gets his hands on your wife and children. He's a monster, and he's seeking the worst kind of revenge."

Orville couldn't believe what he was hearing, but he could tell it was futile to change Hank's mind.

Orville arose from his chair and departed the library with Hank's book.

Orville went back to Herb's and starting looking up the names in the telephone book that matched the surnames of those in attendance at the warlock's execution. He looked at the five-hundred-pound phone and, after taking a few deep breaths, started dialing.

After spending four hours trying to find someone who would believe his story, he threw down the notepad in disgust and began to ponder his fate and the fate of his family and relatives.

At dinner, Orville told everyone at the table what he had learned from Hank and read a number of passages from the book. He left out the details of what this unspeakable monster had vowed at the execution, but stated emphatically that their deaths and the deaths of countless citizens of Ipswich were imminent unless by some miracle they could vanquish the warlock. He confessed that his pleas to enlist the help of the community to accomplish the task were fruitless.

Before anyone could fill in the blanks as to what was to come in only a few days on Halloween, Orville said defiantly, "I have a plan that I believe will stop the warlock, but in order to implement it in the time remaining, I need all of you and anyone else we can find to work day and night to prepare for Eli."

Orville's resolve lifted all of their spirits, and instead of giving up, all five of them vowed to each other to do whatever they could to stop Eli from reaping havoc, not only on them, but on mankind.

Orville went out on the porch and began to sob violently as the others turned in to get some sleep before they began the task at hand. He had fooled them into thinking his plan would work, but in reality, his heart was filled with despair.

In the morning, they were up before dawn to implement Orville's plan.

The days passed, and the family toiled relentlessly. Three of their neighbors agreed to help with the task, but did not believe a warlock was really going to materialize on Halloween. The family hardly stopped to rest in the remaining days. The neighbors went home each day and returned in the morning. It took many trips to the hardware store to gather all the supplies Orville needed for his supposed miracle.

Finally, the dreaded day came, and they continued to work until five minutes before the witching hour. Eli was due.

The only lights in the black night emanated from the barn. Bug wackers sizzled as they had throughout the time they had worked. Dead flies covered the barn floor. Directly in the center of the barn was a huge pit, fifteen feet deep. The ax was embedded in concrete with two tractors resting on top of the slab.

Orville, Pam, Tim, Bobby, Herb, and the three neighbors stood on a platform that overlooked the pit, which was encircled by lightbulbs dangling across its expanse to illuminate every nook and cranny of the floor below.

The family joined hands and began to pray while the three neighbors sucked on three Buds and looked on at what they considered sheer lunacy. The neighbors had decided to stay to get a good laugh and to have another great story to tell to the town folk.

Suddenly, the lights flickered, and the wind sounded like a thousand wolves howling in the black night. A cloud of smoke began to rise from the pit. Orville and the family continued praying as the neighbors dropped their Buds and stared with wonder as the smoke billowed and the beginnings of something not of this earth began to form in the pit.

The eyes bulged in the hideous face, and claws began to reach up from the wormy depths. A shrill, maddening keening sound emanated from the pointed fangs that spread across a demonic grin that iced their souls.

Orville stopped praying and gave the command for everyone to pull down on the ropes they were holding. All complied in unison, and eight larges containers of gasoline that were suspended above the pit tipped over and drenched the monster in mid-metamorphosis. The pit began to fill with gasoline that swept over the head and shoulders of the beast and enveloped it except for the clawed hands that were now completely formed.

All but Orville retreated for the barn door. Orville remained with a torch, which he let fly into the pit. The gasoline ignited into a raging inferno, and the warlock, still only partially formed, shrieked in pain as his eyes darted about the pit and fixed on Orville. The warlock's skin evaporated from its skeleton, and the claws melted into smoldering ashes.

Orville ran to join the others outside as the entire barn was enveloped in flames that rose through the roof and lit up the midnight sky. The maddening shrieks began to subside, and the wind died abruptly as if God had waved a magic wand.

The last thing that Eli saw before both his eyes exploded in flames was a banner nailed to the barn wall that read "Happy Anniversary, Eli!"

The Millers gathered on the porch of the old farmhouse and watched the barn being devoured by the fire. Pam started to pray, and the neighbors from the surrounding farms flooded in to see the burning barn. In no time at all, the walls disintegrated into rumble, and the flies and horrible stench were gone with the warlock.

Orville thought of what he would do the next day and the day after to put their lives back together. He called all the neighbors together for a prayer to give thanks that the devil had been defeated once again.

Suddenly, the charred remains of the tractors and the block of concrete holding the ax exploded in the pit, and a strange whine was heard above the unison of the Lord's Prayer. They all saw a shadow flit across the face of the full moon. One by one, the heads of those whose ancestors participated in the execution of the warlock in 1697 fell to the ground, and blood spurted from their severed necks. The headless bodies flayed at the air and finally toppled to the ground. The Millers and nine others lost their heads that night, while the others stood aghast at the carnage that had taken place. None of the survivors had any idea what had happened. No one saw what had killed the victims who were strewn about the grounds in front of the farmhouse. No one understood why he or she had been spared.

Earlier, just before midnight, Hank Gardner poured a double shot of scotch on ice. He had just written a suicide note with an explanation of the murders that he knew would take place all around the area. He was unaware how far Eli's vengeance would reach. He mentioned the murders at the Millers' farm as the initial murder scene. He thought the mass murders that took place that night might offer some credibility to his story, but thought some other explanation would be presented in the media to avoid what had really happened.

He heard a high-pitched keening sound far away, but gave it no thought as he took his final sip of scotch and placed the glass on the kitchen table. He picked up the revolver, but before he could place it in his mouth and pull the trigger, the window before him shattered in the flash of an eye, and his head and the hand holding the revolver toppled onto the table.

* * *

THE VELVET CAGE

In the heat of a summer's day in 1963, two middle-aged women swayed back and forth on a porch swing in the shade of a great mimosa tree that hung over the antebellum homestead. The grass was green, and the sun was afire as they reminisced happier times.

Mary looked at a little boy who passed on the sidewalk with his big wheel and said, "Joe's a kind man, and he's so good with the children. They love him so. I would have liked to have a career of my own, but when we had three children in three years, I had to settle on being a housewife. It's really been hard on Joe trying to make ends meet with only one income, and college is right around the corner for all three."

"Being a mother is a full-time job, and you really are good at it," Cora said supportively.

"I hardly ever see Joe anymore since he started the graveyard shift. A night watchman is a lonely job, both for him and for me, but in this economy, there's no way to be choosy."

Cora paused for a moment and wiped some perspiration from her brow. "I know what you mean. It's the same with Frank since he got his promotion. He flies off to Chicago or New York almost every other week, and here I sit in this big house alone."

"I hate to say it, but you're very lucky to be married to a man like Frank. You don't have to worry about a lot of things Joe and I never stop worrying about."

"Money isn't everything," Cora snapped. "Sometimes I wish Frank were just a simple man without such strong ambitions."

"I guess I'll never understand you, Cora. You have such a good life, but you're never happy."

"It's hard to be happy when you don't know the person you've lived with for seventeen years. I've never told you this, but sometimes Frank seems like a complete stranger. He comes home, gobbles down his dinner, and then he sits in his big armchair in the den and stares at the wall all night."

"Maybe it's his new position. People who make a lot of money have a lot of pressure on them. What does he say when you ask him about it?"

"He won't talk about it. He just sits there staring. Maybe there's another woman in Chicago or New York."

"Cora, how could you say that about Frank? He's always been so good to you and Millie."

Tears welled in Cora's eyes, and she started to sob. It was apparent to Mary that things were much worse than she had ever imagined.

"Get hold of yourself! It can't be as bad as all that."

Cora grabbed a handkerchief from her purse as she saw Fred and Millie drive up. She didn't want her daughter to see her crying, so she retreated inside the house to freshen up.

Fred and Millie hesitated in the driveway and whispered to each other.

Mary put on her happy face and greeted the teenagers as if nothing had happened. "Hello, young lovers. What have you been up to today?"

Fred and Millie both blushed at her remark and didn't know how to respond. They waved and scurried off toward the back of the house and the swimming pool.

Mary's smile faded as the young couple disappeared behind the house. She waited for Cora to return.

Cora reappeared at the doorway and rejoined Mary on the porch swing.

"Frank has changed, I tell you. We don't talk anymore. He goes his way, and I go mine. He's been going out late at night and coming home drunk."

"I had no idea."

"To make matters worse, I'm really worried that Fred and Millie are getting too serious. They see each other every day at school and after classes, and then he comes for her about four evenings a week. And the way they look at each other when they're together..."

"Oh, Cora, they're young. This is Millie's first romance. Don't you remember when you were their age?"

"I remember too well. That's what worries me. Millie should be dating other boys, but after seeing Fred for more than a year, it looks like she may never have the opportunity. My Lord, she's only sixteen."

"Millie is a good girl, and she'll do what's right. I've got to be going. I need to pick up something for little Joey's birthday."

Cora seemed shocked at Mary's remark. "He's having another birthday. It seemed like only yesterday..."

"He'll be three the seventeenth of the month."

"I wish I could've had another one. They're so cute when they're small."

"But, oh, what a pain," she chuckled as she left through the front gate.

Now that she was gone, Cora was not only worried, but afraid to think what would happen when Frank came home. He had been so mean to her the last few weeks. He'd even slapped her the night before and broken a piece of her precious china when he stormed out. She had tried to be a good wife. She was a good cook, her house was always tidy, and she was more than receptive when Frank wanted to make love.

Frank was off today, and he'd gone out after lunch. She had prepared dinner and put on a little makeup in hopes that things would be better when he came home. She sat in a big armchair and started to re-stitch the hem on one of Frank's dress slacks. Her eyes began to fill with tears. She dropped the mending and laid her head back on the armchair.

A sudden clatter aroused her from a dead sleep. When she opened her eyes, the room was dark. She sensed it was late, but couldn't see the time. A shadow jerked across the room and overturned the lamp on the end table, which came crashing into pieces on the floor. The smell of liquor was strong on his breath as he crawled toward her.

"You've been drinking again," she cried as the tears started to flow once more. "Why, Frank? What's gone wrong with our marriage?"

"You are what's wrong, bitch!" he screamed and lunged for her. His hand grabbed her ankle, and he threw her to the floor. His hands clawed at her blouse as he clubbed her in the face with his fists. Tearing her dress to shreds, he pulled down his pants and mounted her as she writhed on the floor.

"Frank! Stop it! You don't know what you're doing!" she screamed.

"My wife," he shrieked hysterically. "Come, little woman, show me what you can do tonight."

Hours passed. Cora crawled along the floor to the master bedroom and continued into the bathroom leaving a trail of blood across the carpet and tile. Her face and her upper body throbbed with pain from the vicious beating. She lifted herself into the tub and struggled with the hot and cold handles, letting the water run over her. She lay there in what remained of her clothes as the water turned pink from the blood caked on her body.

She heard the sound of a door opening and heard her daughter's voice. "Mom, what's happened? Where did all this blood come from?"

"Don't come in here. Go to bed," Cora ordered. "Don't ask any questions, just go to bed. Your father and I have had a bad argument, and I can't talk now. I'm alright."

Millie paused at the crack in the half-open door and then disappeared into the darkness. She wondered if life would ever be same again after this night.

Frank changed his bloody clothes and combed his hair and drove off toward the city. He could see neon winking in the distance. He pulled into a strip joint. Red devils and pink elephants swam in his head, and the smell of hard liquor and cheap perfume was heavy in the air. He took a seat at the bar and ordered a double bourbon. The bartender eyed him reluctantly, but filled the order.

The girls bumping and grinding on the stage were past their prime. Most were fat and ugly with heavy makeup. They looked at him as an easy mark. It was obvious he was drunk and on the verge of passing out. It was just a matter of time. A platinum blonde with dark roots came up to him and took his hand. She smiled seductively and looked upstairs. He nodded that he was game, and she helped him up the stairs to a seedy room. The world was spinning as he saw her wrinkled, sunken face and felt his wallet leaving his back pocket.

Suddenly, the door burst open and he saw the silhouette of a man standing in the doorway. A naked light bulb blinded him, and he heard the man screaming. The woman in bed with him told the man to get lost. Frank was too drunk to care what was happening and shielded his eyes with a pillow. The two continued to curse at each other as his head began to throb with pain. He heard the thunder of two shots from a gun and felt his chest explode from the impact. He heard the sound of running and more screams as he lost consciousness forever.

Cora sat in her big armchair waiting for Frank to come home. She didn't know how she could ever forgive him for what he had done, but she had nowhere else to go. Her hands trembled as she wondered how to handle the situation. She even blamed herself to some degree for his rampage, but she didn't know what she had done wrong to cause Frank to be so violent. She thought of what she would tell Millie and hoped the neighbors hadn't called the police.

Millie found her in the chair the next morning and couldn't believe how badly she had been beaten. She held her mother in her arms and slumped beside her. Cora patted her on the head as they both continued to sob for a time.

What had happened to the love they had shared? She remembered the birthdays, the Easters, the vacations, the Christmases. She couldn't conceive of how these happy times could ever come again.

"Millie, get ready for school," Cora ordered and looked into her daughter's eyes that were wet with tears. "I don't want you to be here when Frank returns. We have a lot to talk over. He was drunk last night and didn't know what he was doing. He will be sick when he sees what he has done to me. We'll find a way to work things out. I promise you. So go now."

Millie whimpered, but was too distraught to put up an argument. She did as she was told, and after dressing, she left for school. When she saw Fred waiting outside, she ran to him. He embraced her tenderly and brushed the tears from her eyes. He held her close for a few moments, and they headed off toward school.

About ten o'clock, a police cruiser pulled up in the driveway. Mary was consoling Cora and they were having a cup of coffee when they saw the officer approaching. Cora covered her face with a scarf and stood inside the screen as he came to the door. She could see by the look on his face something terrible had happened, and forgetting her bruised face, she ushered him in.

"Are you Mrs. Cora Mason?" the officer said removing his hat.

Cora nodded, too distressed to speak.

"I'm sorry to be the one to tell you," the officer began, "but your husband was shot and killed at the Lady Luck nightclub early this morning."

The officer continued with the horrible details of Frank's death, but the rest of his words fell on deaf ears. Their life was over. That was the bottom line. She sat on the kitchen chair, and the officer brought her a glass of water.

"The great lover," she choked as the officer put on his hat and left by the front door.

Mary put her arms around Cora to comfort her. "Now, now, Cora, sit down and have a good cry," Mary pleaded. "I can't imagine the hurt you must be feeling, and I hope I never will, but you've got to put this behind you and go on with your life. You've got Millie and me and Joe standing by you."

"Get out, Mary!" Cora cried. "Go home."

"Cora, what are you saying?"

"Millie and I will be moving away tomorrow. There's nothing here for me now but bad memories."

"You can't be serious. Don't let Frank's death destroy you and Millie. Where else can you go? All your friends are here. And what about Fred? What will Millie say?"

Cora sprang from her chair and slapped Mary in the face. "Get out, I said. I don't need you or anyone else. And Millie doesn't need Fred. I know what he's after. The same thing all men want."

"No! Don't say that. You're letting your emotions get the best of you. We've always been friends, and you need me now more than ever. I'll get Joe, and we can wait for Millie together."

Cora picked up a pair of scissors from her sewing basket, raised them into the air, and started advancing toward Mary. Mary screamed and ran out the front door.

"Cora, get a hold of yourself!"

"I'm telling you for the last time. Don't bring Joe over here. If you do, I'll kill him!"

Mary screamed and ran across the lawn and disappeared into her house next door.

Cora returned to the big armchair to wait for Millie. The hours passed, and the shadows deepened as the night fell once again. Her eyes stayed fixed on the front door as she sat mending a seam on her tattered dress. A needle pricked her finger, but she felt no pain. The clock on the mantle read midnight when she heard Fred's car pull up in the driveway. Cora darted to the front door and watched them through the tiny peephole in the door as they ascended the steps. She watched Fred caress Millie's hair with his cheek and bring her close to his side for a goodnight kiss.

Cora's eyes widened with frenzy, and her mind snapped forever. She opened the door and stood in the shadows inside. Her breathing grew faster and faster as she stroked the hem of her dress with long, trembling fingernails. The lovers were startled when the door opened so quickly, but when they saw her in the doorway, they smiled nervously.

"Gee, Mom, you sure scared us for a moment. What are you doing up so late? Did you and Dad make up? Are things back to normal?" Millie continued on and on with questions, but didn't wait for the answers.

Cora stood silent as her shrouded eyes glared at Fred and the way he was holding Millie. And then in a fit of rage she lunged at Fred with her bared nails and clawed at his face as she fell upon him and they tumbled onto the grass.

Millie screamed again and again and grabbed her mother in a desperate attempt to protect Fred from the hysterical attack. Fred rolled away, stunned and bleeding.

"Run!" Millie pleaded. "I'll be alright."

Fred hesitated, but Millie lost her grip on her mother as she struggled to resume her unexplained attack on Fred once again. Cora found her scissors in her apron, and she scrambled toward him shrieking madly.

Fred ran to his car and jumped in. The Mustang sputtered for a second and then roared into motion. Cora lashed out with the scissors through the open car window and ripped a large gash in Fred's sport coat as the car thrust forward into the black night.

Millie saw his headlights come on and watched him disappear from her life in a smoky cloud of dust. Cora lay prostrate on the street, clawing at the asphalt with her broken, bloody fingernails. Lights from the adjoining houses winked on one by one.

* * *

Years passed, and the sleepy little town had seen the last of Cora and Millie. Fred knew in his heart he would always love Millie, but after receiving no word from her for five years, he married someone else, and they had two children.

No one knew where Cora and Millie were living. It was as if they had disappeared from the face of the earth. Fred had sent letters to the old address in hopes they would be forwarded, but he never received a reply and finally gave up.

"Millie, your supper is ready," Cora announced as she slid a tray of roast beef, mashed potatoes, and peas through the elongated slot in the door. She put a glass of ice tea through the iron bars of Millie's room and placed it on a ledge.

The beautiful young girl who had lost her boyfriend, Fred, twenty-five years ago lay on satin sheets and velvet blankets dreaming of the wedding day that never occurred. She wasn't young anymore. Her hair was turning gray, and wrinkles had started lining her face. She looked down and saw the plate of food on the floor next to the barred door. She walked over and sat down beside it. She picked up the wooden spoon and, with dainty sophistication, proceeded to dine. Afterward, she placed a linen napkin neatly to her lips, shoved the tray back through the portal in the door, and returned to bed. Millie's room was beautiful and adorned with satin, velvet, crystal, and fine china dolls. She had beautiful things, but all she really wanted was for Fred to come and take her way so they could live happily ever after.

"He'll come, Mother. Maybe tonight," she said with the same anticipation as she had every night for all those years. Through the lace, she saw the windows with cold iron bars and waited to see if she could see a star fall in the heavens. She counted falling stars and listened for Fred's footsteps on the stairs. "How long has it been since he wrote?"

"He hasn't written. Why should he? He can't fuck you anymore, so why should he write?"

"You're lying, Mother! You're keeping his letters from me. I hate you! I hate you!"

"You don't know men like I do. I couldn't bear to see him treat you like your father treated me."

More days passed, and Millie lay in her velvet cage dreaming of sweet yesterdays of long ago and of the wonderful day when Fred would climb the stairs, break down the door, and whisk her back into his arms and his life.

She jumped out of bed and ran to the open window. Her hands slid down the cold iron bars that stood vertically in front of her. She raised the window slightly, and the wind whispered through the crack, foretelling of the winter and the snow that would soon make everything cold and white. The falling leaves drifted past the window, and the thousand stars twinkled in the night sky. The moon looked like a big vanilla wafer dangling in a pool of licorice ebony. The trees sighed in the breeze, and the sounds of the forest that encircled the house crept up the ivy-covered walls and through the bars, touching her lonely heart.

The scent of evergreen seeped into the candlelit room. She loved candlelight. It made the room seem so magical. The cool breeze disheveled her hair as she turned from the window and slipped into the shadows where the light of the moon couldn't penetrate. She lifted the straps of her flowing pink gown and let it drop to the floor. She saw herself in the mirror in the flickering candlelight. She no longer saw the adolescent features of a growing teen, but the mature body of a woman. Lines of sorrow and loneliness had replaced her freckles and her girlish smile. She opened the dresser drawer, took out the creamy smooth negligee she had been saving for her wedding night, and slipped it on. She returned to bed and thought of Fred coming down the aisle on their wedding day. Her gown was ivory, and she was so beautiful, and Fred was so handsome. They embraced and a thousand pink rose petals danced in the summer breeze.

She thought she heard footsteps on the stairs. Or was it just the wind seeping into the cracks and crevasses of the old house and making human sounds? She listened for a long time, but there was nothing to hear but her own heart beating. The wind had gone to sleep and left her alone.

* * *

Summers, winters, and the seasons in between vanished as calendars were discarded each January. The fading years and broken dreams were hard on Millie. She was no longer a young woman; she was sixty years old. Her hair was gray, and her face was wrinkled. It had been years since she had smiled. The mirror was not her friend, and one day she broke it into a thousand pieces with a candlestick.

And then one day, her mother died in the rocking chair on the front porch. Millie was disoriented when there was no dinner.

"Mother," she called. "Where are you? Isn't dinner ready yet?" Again and again she spoke to the silence behind the locked door.

Another night of moon and stars passed slowly for Millie. The pattern of what seemed like a thousand years was finally broken. The sun came up through the pines. Millie lay there on her bed dreaming the same old dream. First, she imagined, there would be footsteps. A heavy tread unlike the steps of her mother. Then a key would unlock the door, and it would creak open. Fred would be standing there smiling. Then he would sweep her up into his arms and kiss her tenderly. He would look into her eyes and tell her how much he loved her.

Fred stood at the grave side by side with his son and daughter while the clergyman tried to comfort the friends who had come to the funeral. Arlene, Fred's wife, had died painlessly in her sleep four days ago, leaving him alone with a big estate and a heavy heart.

Fred had done very well in his business. He was retired with an income stream that would last far longer than he would ever need. He had enjoyed a wonderful life with Arlene, and they shared a lifetime of happy memories together. His children were both happily married and had their own lives far away.

After the ceremony and the gathering at the house were over and all of his friends and family were gone, he pondered what he would do with his life after Arlene. He really didn't have any hobbies, and since they had just moved into a new neighborhood, he hadn't made any friends. He felt so blessed to have lived such a happy and prosperous life, but the one thing that had always haunted him was what had happened to Millie, the girl he had loved as a teen so many years ago. He had loved Arlene with all his heart, but he had never felt the same degree of love he had felt for Millie. His heart ached for Arlene and still at the same time for Millie. Once and for all he needed to find out what happened to her.

He remembered that the post office had said Cora and Millie had moved to a small town called New Market in the Shenandoah Valley. He packed up some things and headed south for Virginia in his Lexus. It was only 250 miles to New Market, and it would be a beautiful ride over the mountain since the leaves were turning at this time of year.

About a half a mile from Millie's house on the outskirts of New Market, a construction crew was building a new road that was to cut through the tip of the property on the south side. The state had sent letters to all the property owners months before concerning the easement necessary for the new road. Cora was one of the few owners who had not responded to their correspondence, and the check they had cut in payment for the strip of land had not been cashed. The matter had to be resolved, and the state official had been instructed to contact each owner before the crew cut the road through the property.

Four more days passed, and Millie was extremely weak and fading in and out of consciousness from lack of food and water. Her throat was so dry her voice had been reduced to a whisper from crying out to her mother.

Suddenly, a sound far away pricked her ears. She listened and tried to cry out, but she could no longer speak. Again, she heard the sound, closer this time. She sat upright, and the wind whispered through the cracked window. She heard another foreign sound and then a creak on the stairs. Her heartbeat began to accelerate.

His name was a prayer singing on her lips. Softly, softly, she heard the sound of someone climbing the staircase. It wasn't Mother. It wasn't the wind. It was a man—a stranger to this place, possibly someone she'd known long ago.

The last step, and now he was behind the door.

* * *

THE FACE

The fear was over. It was just a matter of time. Harry remembered the wonderful years when he was rich and made love almost nightly with some of the most beautiful women in the world. He thought of Rome. Venice. The South of France. Manhattan. So many fabulous evenings dining in the best restaurants. He suddenly had the overpowering urge for a dry Grey Goose martini. The rain peppered the standing water outside the hut. Beads of perspiration welled on his forehead.

Memories returned…

His mother and father had promoted his success starring in countless television and magazine ads from the time he was six years old until the fateful year he became twenty-five. Mirrors adorned every wall of his house. He was the quintessential media face for all the large corporate ad campaigns. Several of the top studios wanted to sign him for an acting career, and he had been holding out for the best offer when it happened.

Fame and fortune had not come without sacrifices. He had never known a normal childhood. During adolescence when chicken pox had threatened his beautiful face, his mother had bandaged his hands to stop him from picking at the sores, preventing any chance of a lifetime scar. He was forbidden to participate in any form of sports activity as a teen or even now as an adult due to the insurance. He'd been educated at home from kindergarten through college to ensure that his face would remain flawless for his commercials. The way he dressed, the car he drove, and his movie star looks attracted members of the opposite sex like bees to honey, and yet he remained a virgin until he was twenty-one years old.

He had been a success in every way and had become a multimillionaire under twenty-five. Lloyds of London insured his face for thirty million dollars. He had a star on the Hollywood Walk of Fame. His beautiful face and body had adorned the covers of every fashion magazine at one time or another, but his favorite cover was for *Money* magazine when he was photographed standing beside a bevy of starlets on his hundred-foot yacht smoking a big Cuban cigar.

He could have had almost any woman on the planet, but he had a serious fetish for kinky sex, particularly with foreign beauties. He was fluent in eight languages, which came in handy when he dated abroad.

Life was filled with obscene extravagances and countless amorous conquests. The world was his oyster until one fateful night in Madrid.

The buxom Italian starlet he had picked for that night's pleasure was very wealthy and, unlike most of the other female selections, had a mind of her own.

She was not into oral sex, and when propositioned to satisfy the whim of the spoiled millionaire playboy, she balked and was insulted by the proposal. After calling her a worthless bitch, she started a flurry of her own name-calling. Harry's knee-jerk reaction to her verbal retaliation led to a hard slap across her mouth, which caused a split lip and a chipped front tooth.

The raven-haired beauty immediately took a vicious swipe at his face with her long nails. His eyes were wild as he pinned her arms and glared at her with the fury of a madman. He ended her screams with a brandy bottle across her temple. Not once, but ten times he battered her beautiful face into a bloody pulp.

His stature in life, her family tree, the prospect of imprisonment, and the loss of fortune meant nothing to him at that moment. The only thing he was concerned with was attending to his precious face. Tears rolled down his cheek and mixed with the blood from the three-finger tear across his right cheek.

The body of a young woman was found a few weeks later floating facedown in the muck that seeped into and around the city dump. The huge rats that made their home in this part of the city had devoured a large portion of the beautiful brunette. The remains that lay on the cold slab in the morgue were a pile of unrecognizable flesh with no means of identification. The only thing that was changed about Harry was the temporary bandage on his cheek and the floor mats in the trunk of his Mercedes that had to be replaced.

Harry's face was slightly marred from the incident, but it was nothing a little makeup could not hide. His reputation remained intact since no one knew that he was the last person who had been with the missing starlet and she had not been identified as the rat-eaten floater.

He tried to take a little time off from his sexual escapades, but the desire for kinky sex could not be quenched no matter how much he masturbated.

Then came the night Harry had imbibed in too many martinis and had a nightcap of grappa. His attaché had bribed the nightclub owner to supply a room for him to sleep it off since his master suite was across town and he had been throwing up repeatedly. Sometime during the night while Harry was snoring loudly and finally resting comfortably, the door of his room opened and a dark-eyed, sullen beauty slid into his bed and mounted him.

Harry awoke the next morning warm and satisfied. He felt the woman's hand on his shoulder, and he began stroking it and babbling to himself as he started to wake up from the long night of lovemaking and intoxication. Dazed and disoriented, he lifted his weary lids and feasted his eyes on the exquisite face of the young Italian woman still asleep in his arms. She was very beautiful. Her hair was flowing ebony. Her rosy complexion and soft mouth that sparkled with beautiful teeth convinced him that his attaché had truly done well in selecting his companion for the evening.

The only mar from perfection was a peculiar chaffing upon her cheek. He had no idea what kind of compensation she expected for the night's pleasures, which he did not remember at all, but after dressing and grooming himself, he took a few hundreds from his wallet and started to put them in her hand. It was then he noticed four partially eaten fingers protruding from the bed linen. He pulled away the sheet and saw that all but her face was riddled with sores and decaying flesh. He gasped for breath as the word stuck in his throat and caused him to swallow hard.

"No!" he cried. "God, no!"

The rain had stopped, and time had returned to the present. He no longer thought about his face. It was a mesh of bandages. He never looked in a mirror. He wept whenever he recalled that day about a month before when a pool of clear water revealed for the last time the remnants of his beautiful face. The woman that shared his bed that night had not been solicited by his attaché. No one knew where she had come from or where she had gone afterward.

Time was all he had left. He must return to his hut. His walk was over. It saddened him that the walk was so short, but there was nowhere else to go in the leper colony.

* * *

FALLING

"It's hard to cry your eyes out at your father's funeral when his passing has made you a multimillionaire," Janet thought as she tried on a smile and admired the Monet over the mantle that would soon be hers. In her opinion, she had played her part magnificently to the cast of three hundred at the ceremony. Half of the vultures had come to the gravesite in order to get a free meal at the Manor.

Her father had been killed in a head-on collision when a drunk driver crossed over into his lane. She couldn't believe he was gone. The huge house seemed like a monastery without his large, booming voice shouting orders to anyone who would listen.

She looked out through the floor-to-ceiling windows at the expanse of the estate that stood on a knoll overlooking the ocean and saw dollar signs. Probate would take time, but soon it would all belong to her.

"I'm going out. Are you all right?" her husband, Brad, asked as he removed his black tie and picked up the car keys from the end table.

"As well as can be expected under the circumstances," she lied. "I'll probably be in bed when you come home, so don't wake me."

After Brad left the estate in his Mercedes, she heard her daughter Melissa playing a video game in the game room. Janet's father was in the ground next to her mother, but life went on at Shell House like nothing had happened. Alfred, the butler, brought her a martini, and she snapped on the news.

Later that night, a bloodcurdling scream startled Janet awake. The clock on the end table read 3:25 a.m. Brad was sitting up in bed with his eyes open shaking violently. She knew from experience he was still falling in his nightmare.

She placed her hand firmly on his shoulder and shouted like she had a hundred times, "Brad! Snap out of it! You're not falling. You're having that dream again."

She steadied him and then clapped her hands in front of his face as loudly as she could. His T-shirt was soaked with sweat as his eyes began to focus.

When he finally stopped shaking and began to breathe normally, he put his arms around her and pushed her backward into the pillows. He kissed her and squeezed her right breast.

She struggled from his grasp. "Brad! It's three in the morning, and I'm definitely not in the mood."

Brad turned on his side and stared at the wall. Janet lay beside him and stared at the ceiling.

The honeymoon was over, and they both knew it. Janet wanted to sleep in a separate bedroom, preferably in a separate state, but she had promised Brad even before they were married that she would be there for him when his dreams were severely traumatic. She hated being a martyr, but she knew how devastating a phobia could be. She once had a bad experience with turbulence on a flight when she was ten years old, and no matter how many therapists she visited, she continued to take a train when traveling rather than a plane, much like the sports commentator, John Madden. It wouldn't be long until she would be out of the relationship, but she was determined to keep her promise until then.

She loathed Brad since she had discovered his infidelity that fateful night three months before. It happened in the middle of the night. She had been sleeping when something glass fell on the tile floor in the living room and shattered into a thousand pieces.

"Shit! Shit! Shit!" Brad shouted when he realized his attempt to sneak into the house without turning on a light in a severe state of inebriation was not working. After standing in silence for a few moments, he fell over a piece of furniture onto the hard tile. He was writhing in pain on the floor when Janet switched on the light. His face and shirt were smeared with gaudy red lipstick, and he reeked of cheap perfume, sex, and booze.

In seconds, he passed out on the floor. She left him there and went to bed, but didn't sleep.

The next morning, Janet had the maid clean up the broken glass and straighten the living room before Brad awoke. She was sunbathing at the family pool all morning to avoid him.

They never spoke of the matter, and consequently, she didn't know what Brad remembered.

A week later, she received photos of Brad embracing various buxom females in several restaurants and hotel lobbies from a private investigator she had hired.

Digging deeper, she hired a CPA to audit their accounts. In a few days, the CPA provided a report showing a series of large withdrawals to vendors she had never heard of. There was also $150,000 in cash missing from the wall safe in the den.

Based on her current accumulation of evidence to secure a divorce, she worried about what Brad would do when he found out. If anything happened to her, Melissa would inherit the family fortune upon her twenty-first birthday. The only way Brad could get the inheritance was if both she and Melissa were eliminated.

The final straw came when Melissa dove off their yacht for a swim and Brad returned to shore without her. He said he was drunk and forgot Melissa had been aboard. It was a long swim, but Melissa had managed it. She was close to hypothermia when she finally reached the dock.

Janet wondered if this was an accident or a premeditated attempt to eliminate Melissa. Brad was not Melissa's father and they had never enjoyed the warmth of a father-child relationship.

Melissa was extremely fond of her real father and was devastated when he and Janet got a divorce when she was ten years old. Janet had tried everything to mend their relationship to no avail.

Janet couldn't prove that Brad was capable of such extreme measures, but somehow, based on the women, the missing funds, and the Melissa incident, she was beginning to think he was not just the sophisticated, pinheaded Adonis she thought she had married, but a calculating fortune hunter whose goal from the start was the inheritance. This is what her father had claimed all along.

She remembered the name of someone her father had hired to take care of a ticklish matter a few years ago. The name was familiar since the surname was the same as the mobster on HBO—Soprano. Her father had pointed out the house where Soprano lived when they were visiting a relative a few years ago.

Janet was shocked to find his name and telephone number with the other law-abiding citizens: John Soprano, 609-324-8986 in Verona.

Her hands trembled as she dialed. The mobster answered on the third ring. "Soprano, who's calling?"

"This is Janet Wright. I'm Henry Atwill's daughter. I believe you did some work for my father a few years ago."

"I'm sorry, Mrs. Wright, I never conduct business on the telephone."

Janet winced and thought how silly she was to call a mobster on a line that could be tapped. "Sorry, Mr. Soprano, I totally understand the need for discretion. I will send you a FedEx package with instructions where we can meet."

She had Alfred send the package asking Soprano to meet her in the parking lot at Pal's Cabin at 3:00 p.m. the following day.

She told him what car she would be driving and the color dress she would be wearing.

Janet arrived early and parked in the location she'd mentioned. At 3:00 p.m. sharp, a man in a business suit pulled up in a Mercedes, got out, and walked toward her car. Janet got out and met Soprano in the parking lot. He extracted a wand from his coat pocket and waved it over her body.

Satisfied that she was not wired, he spoke, "Mrs. Wright, I am surprised that you know about the business I conducted with your father. It was a very delicate transaction that was carried out with the utmost discretion."

Janet relieved him somewhat by saying, "I don't have any knowledge of the business you conducted and have no interest in finding out what it was. I have seen your name in the papers a number of times, always in connection with alleged mob activities."

Soprano looked at her with cold eyes, but let her talk.

"I am desperate to resolve an extremely delicate matter and don't know who else could help me. I only remembered your name because it is the same as the show on HBO."

"It's amazing how much business that show has generated for me," he mused as a smile crossed his lips and his stern manner eased. "Mrs. Wright, I don't know you, and you don't know me. This could be a trap for you or a trap for me. The only way we can do business is through a third party who I can put you in contact with. That way I stay in the clear if anything goes wrong, but I get a small finder's fee for my trouble. Do you understand?"

"Yes, I understand."

"The person I will recommend does not come cheap. He does meticulous work, and consequently, the work is guaranteed once the fee is paid. If you or anyone else rats to the cops, the act will initiate a contract on yourself and anyone else who has been involved in the bust." He paused to think for a moment and then continued. "Oh, one more thing, once the money has been paid, there's no turning back. Whatever the contract is for is what will be executed—nothing more, nothing less. For this reason, you must be sure you really want what you've paid for. Do you understand?"

"Yes, I understand."

"Be here tomorrow evening at ten p.m. sharp. Bring a hundred thousand dollars in unmarked bills in a briefcase. The task you request will determine the amount of money required. You need not fear being robbed. We may be called upon for...shall we say... unpleasant tasks, but we are honorable. That's why your father hired us. Good luck with your future endeavors. I assume we will never speak again."

Soprano returned to his car and drove away.

The next night Janet returned with a briefcase containing $100,000 in cash. The man that met her was not driving a car, but appeared from the far corner of the driveway through some shrubbery. He was dressed in dark clothing with a knit hat that concealed most of his head and a beard that covered most of his face.

The parking lot was dark, and business along the highway was sparse. The man opened the rear door of the car and sat in the backseat. After the wand ritual, a low voice said robotically, "What is the task?"

"My husband is planning to kill me and my daughter and—"

"This is not my concern. What is the task you want completed?"

"I am not a murderer, you need to—"

Again he interrupted, "Why is not my concern. What is the task?"

"The task is to kill my husband, Brad Wright, as soon as possible before he kills me and my daughter. He lives at 3 Maguire Drive in West Orange. He works for the Omar Corporation in New York City."

"Are there any special instructions on how to accomplish this?" the voice said coldly.

"What do you mean?" Janet sought to clarify.

"Do you want him tortured or killed in a special way? Like having every bone in his body broken? Be drawn and quartered? Burned at the stake?"

"You just don't blow his brains out?"

"We're professionals. We will travel to the ends of the earth to fulfill the specific method of execution you desire. Our range of service starts at twenty-five thousand dollars for a local hit and runs up to our Elite Service with everything on it, which costs one hundred thousand dollars. It all depends on what degree of pain and suffering you want the victim to experience and the length of time you want us to spend administering it."

"I don't hate Brad that much. I'm only doing this in self-defense. I think a case of suicide would be the most desirable way for him to die for all concerned. The specifics don't matter. Surprise me. I don't want to know."

The hit man entered data into an iPhone to arrive at the final price. He made a short call, which caused his demeanor to darken.

"Finally," he said dejectedly. "I'm afraid that we are unable to fulfill your request concerning Mr. Wright. There is a conflict, which I am not at liberty to discuss. I am sorry we have wasted each other's time and must advise you that our business proposal is null and void. Please do not attempt to reach us in the future at the risk of bodily harm or death. Any attempt to contact the police concerning this matter will be dealt with in the harshest of terms. Goodnight."

The man opened the door of her car and walked away as fast as he could to where he had entered the parking lot. Janet shouted, "What is the problem? Why can't you fulfill the contract?" but he never looked back.

She pounded her fists on the steering wheel and sat staring into space with no clue as to what she was going to do next. It was clear that Brad had already hired these thugs to eliminate her and poor Melissa. They were bound by some kind of mobster fair-play rule not to make a contract with a victim already under contract. She needed to get Melissa and make a fast getaway to a remote location—hopefully one with a tropical climate.

When she arrived home, she was met at the door by two police officers with long faces. The first officer removed his hat and stated officiously, "I'm sorry to be the one to tell you that your husband has apparently committed suicide. A note was found in his wallet on the street. He said that his life had been a total nightmare and he'd always been a loser and well," the officer paused, "you can read what he said when you're feeling up to it."

"Are you sure you're at the right house?"

"I'm sure. The deceased is Bradley Wright of 3 Maguire Court, West Orange. He worked at the Omar Corporation in the Empire State Building. In fact that's where he took his life."

"What?"

"We don't know how he managed it, but somehow he found a way to get to the highest floor with access to the street and jumped."

"That's impossible. He was deathly afraid of falling. He never took the elevator higher than the second floor, which is where his office is."

"I'm sorry," the officer explained. "I'm just telling you what I was told. A team of investigators has been at the crime scene for several hours. The jump occurred at about nine p.m. The body has been taken to the morgue for the autopsy. The ME says the deceased is definitely your husband, Bradley Wright. Apparently his fingerprints match a set we have in our computer records from when he was arrested for demonstrating as a teenager in 1979."

Janet tried to reason with the officer concerning Brad's death, but his only suggestion was to make a statement at headquarters. When the officer left, Janet rushed inside and turned on the alarm system.

Over the next few weeks, Janet remembered a number of other unsavory characters her father had conducted business with. Brad had also been involved in some of these shady dealings only a few weeks ago, which must have led to his murder.

With her husband dead, she no longer felt that she and her daughter were in imminent danger. It was apparent that someone had already placed a contract on Brad's life before she had contacted Soprano. Since she had never been personally involved in such matters, there was no reason for the mob to come after her. Nonetheless, to be on the safe side, she hired two bodyguards who were both as big as a house to watch over Melissa and herself until the estate was settled. She also hired private investigators to look into Brad's secret life in hopes that it would lead to why he had been murdered.

A few nights later, she was awakened in the middle of the night by the sound of something breaking on the first floor. She called the lead bodyguard, who answered on the first ring.

"What was that noise? Something fell on the kitchen tile and broke. Is everything all right?"

"We spotted an intruder and—"

The voice was interrupted, and Janet heard a gurgling sound on the phone. Then the house was swallowed in blackness.

A different shade of black moved through the bedroom door, and a bright light blinded her as she heard the sound of rushing feet across the carpet. She felt something prick her arm and swooned into unconsciousness.

Janet awoke in a stupor, bound and gagged to the seat behind the cockpit of a small plane. Through the windshield she could see the panoramic view of a mountain range. She immediately gripped the armrest with bared knuckles and began to convulse.

The man sitting next to the pilot looked like the man she had met at Pal's Cabin. "I was wondering when you would come to," he said without expression. "We've been circling this mountain for over an hour, and I want to get home for the fight. I shelled out forty-one dollars for the pay-per-view on HBO, and I don't want to miss it."

Janet continued to shake uncontrollably and was finding it hard to breathe as the horror of the huge mountain loomed menacingly before her. Her fear of flying sent violent tremors to every pore of her body. She tried to scream, but her mouth was filled with rags and taped shut.

"No need to struggle, Mrs. Wright. Conserve your energy," the man said in a monotone voice. "Now that you're awake, we can start some very frightening flight patterns to get your heart pumping. We can even fly upside down and do some curly cues for a while. That should really give you an adrenalin rush."

Janet's eyes widened, and her heart was beating like a jackhammer as she struggled for each breath. The pilot plunged the plane into a series of nosedives.

When the plane leveled out, the voice resonated on the loud speaker, "We strapped Brad to a 'super shot.' That's the thing that lets you freefall a few hundred feet. We let him fall continuously for about four hours at an amusement park. There was no one around, so we just let him scream. He was pretty much a vegetable when we got him to the Empire State Building, but he just wouldn't die."

The pilot motioned to the man who was talking to her, and he grabbed a black bag and started rifling through the contents with an amused look on his face.

He extracted some paperwork and read each word carefully to be sure he was following the contract to the letter. He shook his head in amazement and read the instructions a few more times to be sure.

With a grin that filled his face from ear to ear, he spoke into the microphone, "Your daughter wanted you to know she was truly sorry she had to have Grandpa eliminated, but it was unavoidable. She also wanted me to tell you she really got her money's worth when she saw Brad splatter all over Thirty-fourth Street...but that was nothing compared to what she has planned for you."

* * *

TO KNOW THE END

Harry left his doctor's office with sweat streaming down his face. Weeks of tests had proven the diagnosis correct beyond a shadow of a doubt. He had only days, possibly only hours to live. The streets were crowded, but he felt entirely alone. No one in the world could help him now.

His church was just around the corner, so he took the time to stop there, probably for the last time. Unlike the streets, the sanctuary was entirely deserted. Only God was present within, and he could feel his presence. Every Sunday for years he had frequented the church and almost always had occupied the same pew, the fifth row from the back. He had married his wife there forty years ago.

He had loved his wife then, and he still loved her more than ever. The devotion he had felt on their wedding day had never ceased. Remembrances were many as he sat there looking back into the glorious past, but he knew he shouldn't linger since time was precious; he had none to waste.

He departed the church. His next stop was the flower shop on Beverly. He had known Mr. Sinclair ever since he had moved there, and each day he bought a small bunch of flowers for Mildred. The gossip of the sales ladies was the same as always. The roses were as beautiful as they always were.

He left the shop and purchased the morning paper on the corner, the same as he did every day. He stood there a while and glanced at the headlines. Finding nothing of note, he headed for home.

He usually took a shortcut, which saved him from walking three extra blocks, but today he decided to take the long way home through the park. The birds were singing loudly, and it saddened him to think he would never hear them again.

Finally, he reached the house. So many beautiful memories lingered there. All the happiness of forty years had taken place within those walls.

He placed the newspaper on the kitchen table and descended the steps down to the cellar with the bouquet. The room below was particularly dim that morning, and he turned on the lamp. He noticed that his plants were extremely dry, so he filled a bucket with water from the laundry tub and watered them.

Beside the flower box was an oblong chest of iron, which was decorated with flower petals engraved into the top. He removed the lid on the box and placed the roses inside. A smile caressed his lips as he looked lovingly at Mildred and said, "I brought you some new roses, Mildred. I know you're going to love them. So much has happened today; I have so much to tell you."

He placed the water bucket on the window ledge and climbed into the chest to lie next to his beloved wife of forty wonderful years. He closed the lid, and only a murmur emanated from the coffin. The furnace whirred as a mouse darted across the floor and disappeared into a dark corner. A spider weaved his web across the windowpane.

Days passed. Harry never reopened the casket. Mildred had passed away five years before, and now Harry had joined her in a bond even stronger than their love had been.

* * *

TOOTH FAIRY

Inspector Clancy took another look at the little boy's body on a slab in the morgue right after the medical examiner had completed the autopsy. Just like the others, Boyd Long's two incisors were missing and a crucifix was driven through his heart, which was entered on the death certificate as the cause of death. Like the other five cases, two silver dollars were found under his pillow at the crime scene—the signature of the New York City child killer, the "Tooth Fairy."

After interviewing Boyd's parents, his schoolmates, and neighbors, it was evident that Boyd was a gifted child, well liked by everyone who knew him. Not one person could think of anyone who would have a reason to harm him. The M.O. was the same as the other victims. All were eleven years old. Nothing tied any of the boys to each other. Each had attended different schools in different parts of the NYC metropolitan area, and there was no indication their paths had ever crossed.

No one had seen any suspicious characters in the neighborhood in recent days before the killings. There was no sign of breaking and entering at any of the crime scenes. None of the parents had seen or heard anything unusual during the nights the crimes were committed. Each boy was found murdered in his bed by the parents the morning after.

The case was getting tremendous media coverage, and the commissioner added another team of detectives after each Tooth Fairy murder.

Clancy ran his fingers through his balding head. Reviewing his notes for the fifth time, he asked the ME, "Jack, tell me you've found a clue on this one. Something the fiend left behind I can nail him with."

"Sorry, Clancy, I wish I had better news. It's the identical M.O. No prints on the crucifix. The teeth were extracted after the kid was staked."

"Staked...that's an interesting choice of words. What do you mean?"

"The way the blunt end of the crucifix is lodged in the breastbone, I would say that it must have been hammered into place with a brick or a heavy mallet. Since the crucifix doesn't have a point, no human being could plunge it through the breastbone so deeply without the aid of some kind of...let's say hammer."

"I always assumed each child had been stabbed with the crucifix."

"Hey, this is my first autopsy on a Tooth Fairy victim. Jerry and Fred did the others, but I know for a fact the same type of crucifix was used on all six victims. I'm sure this point was withheld from the media due to the hysteria the image suggests, but it must be in the other autopsy reports."

"I must be losing it; I didn't pick up on this point when I reviewed the first five case files." Clancy looked at his notes in disbelief and continued. "The media should rename the perp 'Vampire Slayer' rather than 'Tooth Fairy.'"

"It does appear the perp thinks he's slaying little vampires."

"That's crazy. Look at this face. I've never seen a kid look more innocent than this one. In fact every one of them look like little angels that have died and gone to heaven. The parents are the same way. They're all model citizens, and they all appeared to be on the verge of a mental breakdown when I interviewed them at the crime scene. I've never seen such genuine remorse from the loss of a loved one since I've been carrying a badge."

"They may all be as pure as the driven snow, but I guarantee you the Tooth Fairy does not think he is killing angels. I've seen a lot of strange things in my thirty years of dissecting stiffs, but I've never performed an autopsy on an eleven-year-old boy with a stake through his heart...I mean a crucifix."

Clancy ran his fingers through the few hairs he had left on his head and put his notebook in his inside pocket. He grimaced a last reply, "I'm beat, and I need to write up a report on the homicide. Call me if you think of anything else."

Clancy left the morgue, found his car, and drove to the precinct.

After finishing his report, he went home to collect his thoughts and get ready for the commissioner's tirade the next morning and the grilling he would have to face at tomorrow's press conference. He could see the headlines now: "The Tooth Fairy Strikes Again."

When he went to bed, he couldn't sleep. He tossed and turned for hours thinking about the six boys lying on the cold metal autopsy tables. A black fog flooded his senses as he studied each of their innocent faces. One by one, the boys sprang upright and looked at him with dead, hungry eyes. He saw the missing incisors and felt their cold, clammy fingers clawing at his flesh. He tried to run, but his legs were like lead. The open wounds where the crucifixes had been lodged were alive with maggots.

He woke himself with a bloodcurdling scream. Turning on the light, he couldn't stop shaking. He got out of bed and took a cold shower and afterward downed about half a fifth of Jack Daniels. He was feeling better when the sun started to rise. He reviewed the murder books of each victim and hoped to find something he'd overlooked.

"Why is the Tooth Fairy removing the incisors and driving a crucifix through their hearts?" Clancy pondered restlessly. "Why are the boys being murdered when they are eleven years old?"

He went to his laptop and logged into the computer at the office, calling up files from previous child slayings. He jotted down each child's birthday and the date they were murdered.

He couldn't believe what he discovered from the exercise. Each boy was murdered within thirty days of his twelfth birthday. He went into his kitchen and pulled the calendar off the wall. He opened the fridge and popped a can of Bud, reviewing the dates of the murders as he took a refreshing swig.

He sat there flabbergasted when he discovered that each murder had occurred on the night of the full moon just before each boy's twelfth birthday. But why? Based on the general population in the NYC metro area, there may have been hundreds of boys reaching twelve who were not murdered. Why did the Tooth Fairy pick these boys to be his victims?

Clancy didn't know what it all meant, but he was sure this was not a coincidence and must be relevant to the case.

The next day he went to the office and jotted down the blood types of the six victims on the same pad as the birthdays and the murder and full moon dates. The next full moon would be on November 16. If the Tooth Fairy followed his previous M.O., he would have almost a month to work on the case before the next kill.

He called Carl Blane, his favorite computer geek at the precinct, to compile a list of all boys in the surrounding boroughs that would reach the age of twelve within the next month. He hoped the list would be manageable so he could stop the Tooth Fairy on November 16.

Days passed and nothing surfaced except for Blane's input. There were seventeen boys who would be twelve years old after November 16.

Unable to fall asleep, Clancy continued to mull over what the medical examiner had said. When he finally dozed off, he dreamed of the final scene in *Rosemary's Baby*, but instead of Rosemary, he was the one who saw the spawn of Satan in the crib and screamed. This was getting embarrassing. Wet with perspiration, he looked at the clock on his nightstand. It was 4:00 a.m.

The nightmare had reminded him that he wanted to follow up on the list of blood types. The next day, he made an appointment to meet with the parents of the first victim.

Clancy took a seat on their sofa. The Madisons sat on the loveseat across from him.

"I'm sorry to bother you again," Clancy began as he pulled out his notebook and extracted a pen from his shirt pocket. "The Tooth Fairy is still at large, but I believe we do have new evidence, which could lead to his arrest."

Both parents looked hopeful, but their eyes revealed that apprehending the monster would not bring their son back.

"Can you tell me what blood type you both have?"

Delores Madison looked puzzled for a second and answered, "O negative."

George Madison answered, "B positive."

Clancy explained, "There are several characteristics shared by all six victims, and I am trying to see if any other similarities exist. Can either of you think of anything peculiar that happened around the time of conception or the time of your son's birth?"

Delores answered this question immediately. "Why, yes. The peculiar thing was that I became pregnant with artificial insemination from a sperm donor. George and I tried for two years and went through every test imaginable without results. The final conclusion was that George's sperm count was too low to impregnate me. Brent was like a miracle to both of us. That's what makes his death so disturbing and so hurtful."

Clancy thought of *Rosemary's Baby* and got up to leave.

"One more thing," Clancy asked. "What was the doctor's name who supplied the donor?"

"His name was Hans Leiber. He was the chief administrator at the Zydeco Clinic," Delores replied.

"He was a strange bird, but totally dedicated to his work. The Zydeco Clinic came well recommended," George added.

Clancy made a note and headed for the door. "You've been very helpful. I'll be in touch if anything new surfaces."

Back at the office, he began calling the parents of the other victims. All of them were under the care of Dr. Leiber at the Zydeco Clinic. All of them had received the same diagnosis of low sperm count from the husband. All had become pregnant by artificial insemination from a sperm donor. All six victims had the same blood type. Unbelievably, it was possible that all six boys, while having a different mother, could have the same father.

Clancy and his partner went to the clinic the next day. The receptionist informed them that Dr. Leiber was on a sabbatical and Fritz Thorn was now the chief administrator.

Dr. Thorn refused to release any confidential information without a court order.

Fortunately, the commissioner pulled some strings and a subpoena was issued. The records were secured from the Zydeco Clinic and taken back to headquarters for review. Three days later, it was confirmed that seven parents were treated by Dr. Leiber and successfully inseminated by a donor.

During the weeks that followed, Clancy was sure that the next victim of the Tooth Fairy would be Robert Craig, who would be twelve on November 26, ten days after the full moon.

On the morning of November 16, Clancy discovered a manila envelope on his desk. Inside, he found pictures of two corpses, each with a crucifix through his heart. The ghastly incisors were protruding from their lips, and their dead, open eyes looked like they were swimming in blood. Both bodies were laid out in a black suit in their own coffin, in what appeared to be loose dirt in some sort of warehouse. One of the pale corpses was Fritz Thorn, the man Clancy and Alexander had met at the clinic; the other he assumed was Hans Leiber, no longer on sabbatical, but dead.

A white piece of paper was enclosed in the envelope. Clancy's hands trembled as he read the very small writing: "The beast will wake on November 26. Tonight, with the rising of the full moon, I must strike, and my mission will be over. No more monsters will be born. The future of all mankind depends on my success. Wish me well, and don't interfere."

The note was signed T.F.

Clancy sat with his mouth agape, pondering his next move. He was to lead the charge in stopping the Tooth Fairy when the sun went down.

Needing to clear his head, he found a bench in the park where he watched throngs of people passing by. Most looked like they didn't have a care in the world.

When he returned to the office, he saw Alexander grinning from ear to ear. "You won't believe what's happened. A middle-aged man was wasted by a taxi at the corner of 38th and Park, and guess what he had in his pocket?"

"What?" Clancy replied, caught off guard.

"A pouch containing a crucifix just like the ones the Tooth Fairy used, a pair of stainless steel pliers, and a roll of silver dollars." Alexander slapped the pouch on the table and continued excitedly. "Can you believe it? The commissioner is going to start popping the champagne bottles about five."

Clancy looked at the items inside and pretended to lock the pouch in his desk for safekeeping. Instead, he slipped it into his pants pocket when Alexander wasn't looking.

"Where did they take the body?" Clancy asked.

"I think they took him to Presbyterian. Who cares where they took him. It's a wrap. Put on your dancing shoes and let's party. Robert Craig is alive and well. No more Tooth Fairy."

"It's great news, but I can't get my mind around it yet. I think someone should still be on surveillance tonight just to be sure."

"I wouldn't want to be that poor slob. He'll miss the party."

"I'll volunteer for the duty. I'm not in the mood for partying," Clancy said, putting on his coat and heading for the elevator.

"Hey! Where are you going?"

"To the morgue. I want to see what the Tooth Fairy looks like," Clancy said as the elevator door closed.

The sun was falling on the horizon as Clancy arrived at Presbyterian. He took the elevator to the basement and made his way to the morgue. He asked to view the body by himself, and the clerk waved him on.

When he slid the slab forward and pulled back the sheet, he saw a middle-aged man who was uncommonly short with a pointed nose and protruding chin. Blood was splattered on his shirt and pants. The victim reminded him of a joker in a deck of Bicycle playing cards, but the sardonic smile had been replaced with a plaintive expression.

As the corpse's eyes stared back at him, Clancy recoiled when he felt a cold hand close around his in a vice-like grip. Pulling away, he was shocked to see the corpse's hand lying limp on the table. As Clancy pulled the sheet over the face, he did a double take. The plaintive look was now a sardonic smile.

Shaken by the weird feeling, he made his way out of the hospital and headed for the Craig house.

As the full moon rose in the sky, he felt the weight of all mankind on his shoulders. He pulled into a parking space across the street and peered up at the bedroom window of the beast.

He removed the pouch from his pocket and extracted the crucifix, the pliers, and two silver dollars from the roll.

He didn't know what tomorrow would bring, but tonight he had to save the world.

* * *

THE DARK RETURN

Boom! Boom! Boom!

The ring. The crowd. The blood. The count.

Boom! Boom! Boom!

Flashes of explosions filled the night as Ray's mind began to spin and the dream returned as soldiers darted about and machine guns roared.

The painful memories of his last fight and the war continued to haunt him with a vengeance as he pondered the future.

Ray Davis, the heavyweight champion of the world, had discarded fame and fortune at the pinnacle of his career to serve his country in Desert Storm. Unfortunately, the unselfish act had backfired when he had run away on the field of battle and received a dishonorable discharge for cowardice from the army.

It was all a misunderstanding. He wasn't a coward. He knew what no one else knew. The dream. The horrible taunting nightmare was the reason he had run away. The eyes. They were what haunted his every moment. He had recurring dreams that would come upon him without warning any time of the day or night since the fight with Joey Ramos. Joey, who had been his best friend all through high school, had become his rival for the heavyweight championship. They had gone through everything together personally and professionally. Ray had been best man at Joey's wedding only a month before the fatal night.

A vicious uppercut had ended Joey's quest for the championship and his life. Ray could still see his open eyes staring up at him from the canvas. These were the eyes that wouldn't let him forget.

He was back home now, but his war was not over. It was just beginning. He was branded a coward, and nothing in life mattered but rising above the humiliation and regaining his former dignity, not only as a boxer, but also as a man.

He began training with a fury that he'd never known before. He ran and sparred from morning to night until his body was rippling with pure muscle. After seven fights, he had garnered seven more victories; five were won by a knockout. He was undefeated in forty bouts in his career with thirty-four knockouts.

Ray had easily regained his stature as a champion in the ring, but he was still a coward in the minds of the people, who booed him mercilessly from the moment he entered the ring until he returned to the dressing room.

He decided to have one more fight. Even before he enlisted to go to Desert Storm, achieving the belt of the heavyweight champion of the world was no longer important. Joey's death had shattered all his hopes and dreams that fatal night. The only thing that mattered now was removing his brand of a coward in the eyes of his former fans. No matter how many fights he won, he knew they would never forgive him for running away on the field of battle. He pondered his fate and what he must do to make himself a hero once again in their eyes.

Ruefully, he planned the sacrifices he thought were necessary to achieve redemption both in and out of the ring.

Weeks vanished into time, and the long awaited match was only minutes away. The crowd was mixed with catcalls and boos as he left his dressing room and headed toward the ring. The unforgiving crowd grew louder as he stepped through the ropes. He looked out into the expanse of the arena and the teeming spectators and saw one fan waving from an empty bank of seats in the upper deck of the arena. Ray returned the wave as a tear rolled down his cheek.

He paced his corner. The contender, Tony Bastille, glared at him with the eye of the tiger, but Ray's cold stare met the challenger's with a fury he'd never seen before from any opponent.

From the first bell, the two warriors battered each other relentlessly for six rounds. The judges had the bout even on all three scorecards.

In the middle of the seventh round, Ray unleashed a vicious left hook followed by a pile-driving right cross that sent Bastille to the deck. He was unconscious and not moving for part of the referee's count to ten, but Ray was happy to see him trying to stand as the announcer made his way into the ring after he was counted out.

The crowd was booing as Ray stood in the middle of the ring and the announcer began to declare the winner of the contest. As the referee lifted Ray's arm in victory, a shot rang out from the upper deck of the arena. The bullet struck Ray right between the eyes and splattered the referee and the announcer with his blood and gore. Ray's body hurtled backward from the impact of the shot and eerily took the shape of Jesus without the cross on the canvas.

The booing ceased and a hush fell over the arena as the spectators stood in awe at what they had witnessed. Shortly thereafter, the media, the challenger, and both fighters' handlers rushed into the ring, and a state of chaos prevailed inside the arena for about forty-five minutes.

Someone draped some towels over Ray's body until the medics arrived with a stretcher and a gurney.

As Ray's body was being removed from the ring, the announcer finally declared that Ray Davis was still the undefeated heavyweight champion of the world.

After a slight pause, the crowd began to clap slowly at first until the applause increased in participation and volume to a thundering standing ovation.

* * *

TOMMY

Just like every other Friday, Pat Stevens came to visit the grave of her little boy, but today was different. This morning she discovered she was pregnant. She couldn't believe her eyes when the test strip had turned blue. It was a miracle, and to be sure, she performed the test a second time with the same result. She couldn't wait to tell her husband, Frank, the incredible news when he came home from work.

After trying to conceive for more than two years and seeing four specialists, who all concluded she was physically unable to have a child, she had fallen into a deep depression. She and Frank argued constantly about adopting a child, but she was adamantly against it.

After a period of barely speaking to each other, Pat told Frank that she would put the past behind her if he would agree to honor the memory of her only child with a gravesite at the nearby cemetery. She explained that the child from her first marriage had died at birth and they were so poor the city had taken care of disposing with the body. Since she was so distraught she could not have another child and the creation of the mock gravesite seemed to placate her, Frank gave in to the bizarre request.

The cemetery was just a short walk through the trees from where they lived. She was proud of the site, which had a small plaster statuette of a baby angel for a headstone. Engraved on the face of the marble plate were two words: "Our Darling." Each time she came to pay her respects, she wondered if she was the only one in the cemetery who was visiting a grave that had no body.

She found a nearby bench, and despite her newfound joy of being pregnant, she couldn't erase the guilt of what had really happened to her first child.

The real truth was that her first child was the result of a gangbang by most of the members of her high school football team when she was fifteen. She had no idea who the father was and was never married before she met Frank. Unfortunately, the baby was delivered after a C-section, which created the need to fabricate the previous marriage.

Her parents were God-fearing Christians who would not allow her to have an abortion. When the baby was born with horrible birth defects, her parents told her that God was punishing her for having sex with so many boys out of wedlock.

She named her son Thomas Eastwood because Clint was her favorite actor. Tommy was nothing but trouble. No one could understand a word he said because of a severe hair lip. His face was so grotesque that children wouldn't stay in the same room with him. Pat knew she could never live a normal life with Tommy. He needed expensive special care, and no man would have anything to do with her once he saw him.

When she was twenty-four, Pat decided to start a new life in Baltimore. It was far enough away from home, and she thought she might be able to hook up with a gangbanger who had moved there a while back. She packed two small suitcases and left with Tommy in a rental car. It was Sunday and her parents had gone to Church. She left a farewell note on the kitchen table for them that read, "Kiss my rosy red ass, you miserable hypocrites."

After driving about twenty miles on a country road, she turned off on a dirt road and finally pulled into a clearing with the remnants of a deserted well. She had stopped there many years ago on a picnic with some gangbangers.

It looked a lot better then, before the weeds had overtaken everything.

"Tommy, do you want to make a wish at the wishing well?"

"What's a wishing well?" Tommy mumbled.

"Come with me and I'll show you!"

They made their way through the weeds to the wishing well.

"Here's a penny. Go to the well, close your eyes, and make a wish."

Tommy obeyed.

"Now climb up on the edge and throw the penny into the well."

As Tommy leaned over the lip to throw the penny, Pat lifted his feet and threw him head over heels into the gaping mouth of the well.

After a long silence, she heard the sickening thud far below. She wondered what he had wished for as she drove away.

Ten years later, the guilt of killing her own child was still haunting her. She still had horrific nightmares that caused her to wake up screaming. Spending a little time at the gravesite each week helped ease the guilt of that unspeakable act so long ago.

Today seemed like every other day when she walked up. Reaching down to place the red roses on the grave, she was shocked to see a bouquet of fresh lilies already in the vase below the headstone. She also noticed that the grass atop the grave looked like it had just been resodded. As she removed the lilies and replaced them with her roses, she saw the name engraved in the marble. Directly under the words "Our Darling" was "Thomas Eastwood, September 8,1992–October 31, 2000." Her head began to spin, and she slumped to the ground.

Pat awoke at dusk. She struggled to her feet and brushed some grass from her skirt. She stared at the headstone in disbelief.

Who could have done this? She had changed her name and spent a considerable amount of money to create a new identity.

Her parents were dead, and she had lost contact with all of her relatives long ago. She didn't attend her parents' funerals and did not inquire about any inheritance she may have been entitled to. Her son's name was something she made up after the birth certificate was filed without a given name. She was confident that fingerprints and DNA evidence would be useless in connecting her to the dead body even if it were found. If they did trace her, why had the police not arrested her?

She called Frank and asked him to drive to the gravesite. She thought about telling him she was pregnant, but decided it should wait.

He considered her request as insane, like everything else about the fictitious gravesite, but knew he would always humor her. He loved Pat dearly and did what he could to make her happy.

In a few minutes, he pulled his car into the parking space next to hers. When he joined her at the grave, he was immediately puzzled by the name on the headstone.

"Did you give the boy a name and have someone engrave it on the headstone after all these years?" Frank questioned.

"Of course not. I have no idea who did this or why. They even put lilies on the grave. I wondered if you knew anything about it."

"I don't know anything. I guess the only answer is that someone who doesn't have any money has buried his kid in our cemetery plot."

"How could anyone think they could do this without repercussions?"

"I'll notify the police and let them take care of it."

"No! I don't want to get the police involved," Pat stated emphatically. "Let's start with the cemetery administrator. Let him look into the situation before we involve the authorities."

The next morning, Frank called George Landers and informed him of the bizarre mishap.

After waiting on hold for a few minutes, Landers said, "I assure you, Mr. Stevens, that no one has been buried in the Queen of Angels section for over a month."

"Maybe not officially, but certainly illegally. It probably happened in the middle of the night," Frank responded gruffly. "The grave has been violated, and a name we don't recognize has been engraved on our headstone. What are you going to do about it?"

After pausing for a few moments, Landers responded irritably, "We will exhume the casket and examine the contents if you give us written permission."

"When can you do it?"

"Tomorrow morning at ten o'clock."

"We'll be there.

The next morning, Frank and Pat watched the bobcat remove the dirt. Three workmen shoveled until the casket was uncovered and raised it to ground level. They placed a canvas enclosure around the casket and removed the top for viewing.

Frank and Pat stood agape. It was not a freshly interred body their eyes fell upon, but one that had been decomposing for a considerable period of time. A bluish-gray layer of putrefying flesh stretched across the skeletal frame, allowing some degree of human recognition.

Pat stifled a scream when she saw the hair lip that disfigured the small face. The right arm of the corpse was twisted at a familiar odd angle. She remembered how her son's backbone extended higher than the neck. There was no doubt this was Tommy, not someone else's child.

Frank caught Pat in his arms as she started to fall.

"This is not a new burial," Landers stated meekly, wondering if he should remain silent. After a moment, he added, "Forgive me for asking, but are you sure this is not your child after all."

"I'm positive it is not my child since we buried an empty casket without a body."

Landers looked at the distraught man incredulously and waited for an explanation.

"My wife had a child who died at birth during a previous marriage. We purchased the gravesite, and even the casket, as a kind of belated memorial to his memory."

"Who is Thomas Eastwood, the name on the headstone?" Landers asked.

"We have no idea who he is."

After Pat regained consciousness, Frank escorted her to the car and asked Landers to wait there until he returned from taking his wife to their house, only a few blocks away.

When Frank and Pat arrived home, Pat confessed that she hadn't told him the truth about why she wanted the gravesite. She told him that when she was a young girl she had a deformed child who wandered off into the swamp and was never found. She named him Thomas Eastwood. She left out the part that she had murdered her own son.

Frank responded, "And you think that someone has gone to the trouble of placing your real son's body in our empty casket and putting his name on our gravestone?"

Pat started to sob uncontrollably. Frank consoled her as best he could and promised everything would be all right. Pat rested her head on the sofa, and Frank left the house to return to the cemetery, where Landers and his crew were waiting for a decision.

When he arrived, he found the casket lying askew across the open grave. Landers's dead body was stuffed into the small casket. His head was smashed in on one side. The workmen had disappeared.

Frank saw a young boy's footprints in the damp earth that led off in the direction of their house.

Frank picked up the shovel that was lying by the grave and hurried into the woods toward his house. The sun was going down, and the rain clouds were ominous.

The front door was standing open as he rushed inside, shovel at the ready. The only sound was the hum of the refrigerator.

It was dark as thunder rumbled in the distance. He snapped on the living room lamps.

He saw a trail of muddy footprints on the carpet heading up the stairs.

"Pat?" Frank called out.

Silence.

Frank heard the sound of something shuffling across the floor upstairs and immediately took the stairs, two at a time, to the second level.

He rushed into the master bedroom and saw Pat cowering in the far corner. What was left of the decomposed body was shuffling toward her with its skeletal hands outstretched.

Frank plunged the shovel into its neck, sending the head flying across the floor. The headless body continued toward Pat, who was screaming at the top of her lungs.

Frank plunged the shovel through its back, which pushed the putrefied intestines out through its stomach. The corpse's body doubled over and collapsed to the floor. Frank saw the dead eyes in the wormy head still glaring at Pat with animal fury. Frank continued to plunge the blade of the shovel into its writhing body until it stopped moving.

He rushed to Pat's side and embraced her.

When things had settled down for the night, Pat told him she was pregnant. He kissed her tenderly, and the horror of the day was replaced by the promise of the future.

The authorities closed the case without resolution. No one believed Frank and Pat's story about the corpse reanimating itself. The identity of the corpse remained a mystery, and there were no leads on who killed the cemetery administrator, George Landers.

Eight months later, the happy day arrived. When Pat's water broke, Frank drove her to the local hospital without complications. The delivery was textbook. Pat had experienced much less than normal labor pains, and even the duration of the birth was uncommonly short.

When the head and then the shoulders came out of the birth canal, the pediatrician removed the boy, wrapped him in linen, and laid the baby on Pat's stomach. Frank beamed with the wide grin of a proud father as he pulled back the little sheet from the baby's face to take a look.

Pat saw Frank's smile evaporate in an instant. His face contorted in horror. She lifted the baby from her stomach and turned it toward her. Frank rushed to her side as the doctors and nurses stood aghast at the sight of the infant's deformed head.

Pat's piercing scream was like fingernails across a blackboard.

The baby looked a lot like Tommy.

* * *

THE STRANGER

A soldier made a call from a phone booth in the Trenton train station.

"Hello, Dad. I'm home. My tour of duty is finally over. How's Mom?"

"She's fine, and we're all here at the house. I'm making margaritas. It's Friday night and we're ready to party. We can't wait to see you."

"Gee, that's swell. A party, huh? I guess a man's got to get his mind off what's passed and learn how to live again." The soldier hesitated for a moment and said, "Sure, Dad. Let's have a party. It'll be just like the old times."

"Take a cab and get your butt on over here."

"Dad, there's something I need to ask you. I have a friend who had a bad break and lost his leg in the fight. His mom and dad are dead, and he doesn't have anywhere to go. I was hoping he could take Junior's old room and stay with us."

"Do you mean indefinitely?"

"I haven't thought that far ahead. It's Christmas, and I know how much fun we had as a family this time of year."

"Is he with you now?"

"No, he won't be discharged until next week. I didn't want to spring him on you without getting your approval first."

"I'm sorry, Son, but your mom has been ill and she can't cook and clean like she did before you enlisted, and I'm afraid that, due to the economy, I'm going to be laid off. We're not set up to care for your friend."

"Sure, Dad. I know Mom's been sick lately, and you've been talking about being laid off for the last twenty years. Really, he's been rehabilitated and has been taught to take care of himself. He won't be any trouble, I promise."

"We really don't want a stranger in the house at this point in our lives. It's so awkward to make conversation at the dinner table. Who knows what kind of TV shows he likes. How loud he plays music. I know you want to help your friend, but it's a lot to take on, particularly in light of his disability."

"Trust me, Dad. My friend is so much like me; he won't be a bother at all. He likes all the TV shows we watched before my deployment."

"We want to help, and we'd love to put him up for a few days, maybe even a week, but we don't want to make a long-term commitment. We just don't want a stranger living with us."

"A couple of days. Sure, Dad. I understand. I know he's got to face the world sooner or later. Better sooner than later, I guess."

"Are you on your way? The burgers are almost ready."

"Home? I won't be long now, but I need to take care of a few things first. I won't be long. Take care of yourself, and tell Mom I love her. Goodbye."

"Son! Wha—"

The soldier hung up the phone. Tears rolled down the young man's face as he left the phone booth and moved slowly off into the shadows outside the train station and toward the taxi stand. If only he did have a friend. If only he weren't the stranger who had to learn to face the world…alone.

* * *

SHADOW ON THE STAIRS

My name is Conrad Twist. I am a total loser. Webster and his descendants could have used my picture in their dictionary to show the world what a loser really looks like. I have accomplished nothing I set out to do when I graduated from Yale.

I have been a nursemaid to my sister, Emily, as a condition of the will since my father, who I nicknamed "Hitler," and my slut of a mother were wasted in a head-on collision. Emily has been confined to a wheelchair with muscular dystrophy since she was eight years old. My aunt Sue and her worthless husband, Tom, are also living here in the lap of luxury afforded us by our father's vast money-laundering empire.

I have to give my father credit for recognizing that I have no ambition to follow in his footsteps. Why bother when I could never match the lifestyle I already have by doing nothing? Nonetheless, I hate my father for his good judgment concerning my character in putting me under Emily's thumb.

It's been a living hell waiting on Emily hand and foot for the past ten years. The only salvation is I am to inherit everything when Emily croaks. Unfortunately, Emily has been writing large checks to the "Save the Polar Bears" foundation, which has been severely depleting the funds that would eventually be mine.

The doctors have said repeatedly that Emily would probably not live more than a few more years, but what if they're wrong? I remember an old Hitchcock show where the hot babe marries a filthy rich geezer who was also supposed to die in a short time. Each year on the anniversary of their marriage, the geezer rolled a pearl across this long table to his wife, and after many years, she had a necklace of pearls. Since the old geezer wouldn't die, the young wife and her lover, who had been waiting in the wings all those years, decided to eliminate the old reprobate. And so I have come to the same inevitable conclusion as the gold digger in Hitchcock's episode: I must kill my sister, Emily. Tonight is the night I've been waiting for so long.

She has treated the three of us like dirt from the start, and I don't think she cares if there is anything left for us once she's gone. Sue and her worthless husband probably assume they will continue the same lifestyle when Emily is worm bait, but I assure you, this will not be the case.

I can't wait for the magic hour. It will be the most fun I've had in ages to see the surprise on her twisted face when the wheelchair goes crashing down the long spiral staircase. I can almost hear her bones crunching on the beautiful mahogany treads now. Hopefully, there will be some blood. I can't wait to replace that horrid green carpet.

I spent the day doing crosswords and Sudoku until the time came. Tom and Sue were at the dinner table, and it was time for me to bring Emily down in the elevator, which had been added when Emily was confined to the wheelchair.

She was waiting in her room with her usual overbearing manner and her ugly blue robe. Her hair was askew, and a bit of drool glistened at the corner of her mouth. Without ceremony, I guided her wheelchair toward the elevator, which was conveniently located at the top of the spiral staircase.

A faint scent of body odor hung in the air as we approached the elevator—and the stairs. And just like clockwork, she started talking about the polar bears and their horrible plight. The icecaps were melting, and they were having trouble swimming to their food supply. This was like chalk on a blackboard to my fragile senses. I could bear it no longer. I pretended to trip and with all my might thrust out my arms, and the wheelchair went plummeting down the stairs. About halfway down, Emily's head conveniently careened off one of the treads, and blood splattered upon the wall and left a trail all the way to the foyer floor.

I lay there prostrate on the floor writhing in mock distress and pounding my fist into the rich mahogany floor. I was sobbing with enormous conviction as Tom and Sue appeared in a run.

"My slippers slipped out from under me when I reached the elevator and she went over!" I screamed.

Tom and Sue were standing below, visibly shaken by the sight of Emily's bloody corpse. Her vacant eyes stared up at me at the top of the stairs. Her front teeth were crushed in, which made her look even more hideous than usual.

"What have I done?" I said leaning against the banister. I masterfully hid a smile that I couldn't quite control in my sleeve and continued to snivel violently.

Tom ran to the phone and called 911. Sue slumped to the floor and continued to weep with conviction until the police arrived.

After what I thought was an academy-award-winning performance, all concerned considered it a terrible, unfortunate accident. The police were undoubtedly fooled by my performance, but even though silent throughout the investigation, Tom and Sue didn't seem as convinced I had slipped.

Emily's body was hauled away like a side of beef on a stretcher. The term "meat wagon" crossed my mind as I saw the ambulance pull away.

"How appropriate," I mused.

After Emily's body was removed, a peculiar dark outline of where she had come to rest remained on the carpet. The outline resembled a shadow, but with further inspection, there was nothing to cast the shadow. It was a creepy turn of events, but I tried not to let it ruin what had up until then been a perfect day.

A carpenter cleaned and waxed the hardwood treads, and the staircase looked as good as new. Mysteriously, even after the carpet people installed a beautiful red carpet, the dark spot remained. Everyone who came to the house during the investigation said they thought the outline looked like a shadow. I had that piece of carpet replaced, but still the shadow remained.

I moved my room to the other side of the house to avoid coming into contact with the shadow.

Weeks passed and the will was finally read. It was confirmed. I was to inherit everything. Tom and Sue were to be the next in line upon my demise. I pretended to be surprised at what I had known all along.

The next day, I told Tom and Sue to vacate my house as soon as possible. Of course, they hated me for throwing them out in the street after so many miserable years together. A week later, I was finally free of the whole family. The entire estate was mine!

After they left, I made a list of all my possessions. I reviewed all my bank accounts, stocks, bonds, etc. I lit an expensive cigar and poured myself an expensive cognac. I sat there for hours and knew that I could be the happiest man on earth.

Suddenly, I thought I heard Emily's voice. I looked around and saw nothing. I called out, and there was no answer. I was so rattled; I returned all the important papers and checkbooks to the safe in the living room that was hidden behind an ugly portrait of Emily, Tom, Sue, and myself. I composed myself and searched the house, but after two times around the first floor, I found nothing suspicious. The only sound in the huge house was the crackle of a burning log that I had placed in the fireplace when I was tabulating my great wealth. I was about to search the bedrooms upstairs when I came to the bottom of the staircase and found the shadow on the carpet had disappeared. A chill ran up my spine as I looked about. My heart was beating like a racehorse when I spied the shadow in the middle of the staircase. I felt extremely dizzy and stumbled backward and slumped on a sofa at the base of the stairs.

I awoke sometime in the middle of the night. There were only embers in the fireplace, which was the only light in the house. I turned on a lamp, but it appeared the power was out. I proceeded up the stairs with a flashlight to see if the shadow was still there in the middle of the stairs. It had disappeared.

I moved to the top of the stairs and surveyed the carpet. There it was. The same as it had been at the base of the staircase. The image of Emily's dead body materialized before my eyes and filled the shadowy outline. I dropped the flashlight and let out a piercing scream. A green glow emanated from her body, reminding me of the horrible green carpet I had replaced. I ran down the stairs and tried to exit through the dining room. The dining room chandelier started to flicker. The thing that looked like Emily stood in the doorway with a hideous grin that curled around broken teeth. The apparition was blocking my escape from the house. She pointed a gnarled finger at me and beckoned me toward her.

I took the elevator to the second floor. When I left the elevator, Emily's animated corpse reached out for me. I backpedaled away as her menacing fingers reached for my throat. With gnashing, bloody teeth and bulging, dead eyes, she slithered toward me, one foot dragging behind the other. I screamed in horror as I plunged backward and dove headlong into the abyss that was the spiraling stairway. My head cracked on the mahogany treads several times during my descent, and one eye exploded from its socket before I landed in a crumpled, broken heap at the bottom of the stairs.

With my one good eye, I saw her standing in the shadows at the top of the stairs, and I heard the unpleasant shrillness of uncontrollable laughter. Descended the stairs, she stood over me and seemed to savor each of my final gasps for breath. The hellish figure placed her hand on the top of her head and pulled off an incredibly authentic, hideous mask of Emily. I immediately recognized Aunt Sue standing there in a glowing version of the dress that Emily had worn to the grave. The lights came back on, and I saw Tom step into view as I began to lose consciousness.

I heard the pop of a champagne cork, which was followed by uproarious laughter and the intermittent commentary on how laser images and holograms had done the trick in scaring me out of my wits. They were so happy that I fallen down the steps to my death, as they had hoped, which didn't require them to commit the dirty deed directly. I lay there in a grisly heap as my miserable life went through my mind in a really neat pictorial display.

It was clear that my back was broken since I couldn't move a muscle. My neck was twisted at an odd angle, but my head was propped up against the final tread at the bottom of the stairs, which left me in the perfect position to see my blood oozing into a pool on the floor with my one good eye.

I wondered if they would repair my missing teeth, my ruptured eye, and my lopsided head before the funeral. Or would there be a closed casket?

* * *

PATHS OF GLORY

The tiny orb shattered in midair, and a roar of applause resonated from the crowd. Edwards was an expert in skeet shooting, and this contest was yet again another triumph.

He had won top honors in every form of marksmanship.

Edwards was a haughty man and loved to boast about his prowess whenever the opportunity presented itself. Unfortunately, he had never attempted big game hunting, which was the pinnacle of his art. After winning all other feats of marksmanship, this was next on his agenda.

Edwards had been contemplating a safari into the Congo for more than twenty years. In all his dreams, he was a hero. Each venture ended with him being photographed with his foot atop the carcass of Bengal tiger or an African lion.

He longed to make these dreams a reality. It would be a duel between the brains and the brawn. He thought of gladiators in the Coliseum in Rome, the crowd cheering as they witnessed a clash of titans in the arena of blood and sand. He could see it all now in his mind's eye: the mighty head of a bull elephant fixed in the crosshairs of his British Enfield and the collapse of his prey at his feet, gasping and tossing until the law of the jungle ended the last remnants of its petty existence. He would walk away unscathed, and the splendor of the kill would exalt his name throughout the journals of the modern world. He would be "Edwards the Magnificent, the Great White Hunter."

Finally under the African stars, he lay with the troupe of fifteen he had hired to accompany him on his maiden voyage into the bush. His thoughts drifted to what was certain to happen the next day. Distant tribal drums throbbed in the blackness of the dense jungle. The cries of the beasts of prey increased with the dawn as Edwards and his band left their campfire and sliced their way through the underbrush. Eventually, a ray of light emerged from the dense terrain, and the party looked out upon an expanse of a grassy plain.

Edwards knew this was the battleground he had been dreaming of.

The wind tossed the tall grasses to and fro and made the hunt much more dangerous than he had imagined. He peered into the distance with his rifle at the ready. The sun was hot, and the members of the tribe he had hired grew restless as the day wore on.

Suddenly a maddening shriek roared across the plain, and the thunder of mighty hoofs shook the very earth. Edwards and his band stood motionless as they watched a defiant bull elephant emerge from the underbrush, prodding and heaving its twisted trunk. It was obvious by its appearance that this mighty beast had survived many seasons of battle, as its hide was deeply marked from old wounds and its tusks were disfigured with many combat scars. Edwards was ecstatic; this would be the first animal that would feel his wrath.

He could visualize the mammoth head affixed to the wall in his den as he crept into position.

With his rifle poised to fire, he strode into the field where the male elephant was stomping about with the savage anticipation of challenging another rogue. But instead of finding a formidable member of his own species to do battle with, his eyes fixed on Edwards, the puny man-beast who came ambling slowly but surely toward him. Edwards stopped and surveyed the situation. The mighty elephant stood his ground, shaking his head, seemingly preparing for the optimum moment to charge.

And then with a shattering trumpet blast, the rogue thundered toward Edwards.

Edwards raised his rifle and aimed for the hump right between the elephant's eyes. A torrent of sweat welled in his eyes and blinded him. His hands trembled, and his throat became parched in an instant. The distance between Edwards and the mammoth beast grew less and less. Edwards tried to steady the rifle. The crosshairs shifted to and fro upon the elephant's head. The projecting tusks and the thundering hoofs unnerved his senses. A wild shot missed its mark and careened off a tree to the right of the charging elephant, who was unperturbed by the feeble discharge of the challenger's rifle. The enormous beast's tusks impaled Edwards midsection in an instant as the lower part of his body was crushed underfoot.

The conflict, lasting less than a mere ten seconds, had ended and the result was that Edwards's bloody remains were strewn across a small section of the enormous grassy plain like a drop in the ocean. The hunter was dead, horribly slaughtered by the rogue elephant that knew no master and was oblivious to fear. So it would be until another came to challenge his throne. After the elephant disappeared into the underbrush, the shocked members of Edwards's party who had witnessed the carnage gathered up the remains of their leader on a stretcher.

They buried the pieces of Edwards that they found in a shallow grave and placed his rifle in the ground as a headstone.

There would be no headlines of glory for Edwards; there would be no elegy for his memory. The only trace of Edwards was the rifle that marked his grave, and several of the natives in the party would certainly abscond with that once the sun went down. By morning there would be no trace of Edwards in the ground since what was left of the body would be tonight's nocturnal snack for the jackals.

* * *

TURBULENCE

After winning the lottery for $32 million, I called my boss and told him where he could stick my vice president position at Hemisphere Bank.

I had decided to start celebrating with an around-the-world tour. This had always been an item on my bucket list. My first stopover was San Francisco en route to Hawaii.

Due to a lifelong bout with asthma, I made arrangements for a portable oxygen device to be supplied by the airline for the flight. When I took my seat in first class, the flight attendant hooked me up to the oxygen machine.

I ordered a Martini and started reading the airline travel magazine. After a half hour elapsed, the plane took off, and once the correct cruising altitude was attained, the fasten-seat-belt light was turned off. The flight was scheduled for seven hours, which I knew would not be pleasant, but I was giddy with the excitement of being a multimillionaire. The reading and the cocktail made me drowsy, so I closed my eyes and started to fantasize about how I would spend my $32 million.

In the midst of having sex with a harem of buxom beauties on my magic carpet, the plane suddenly hit a violent pocket of turbulence and jolted me awake and back to reality. My seat belt was already fastened when the pilot's voice came over the intercom.

"Please return to your seats and fasten your seat belts; we're in for some turbulence for about fifteen minutes. There's no need for alarm, and we will make every effort to arrive on time."

I could feel the plane accelerating into a higher flight pattern.

Looking around me, I saw the worried faces of the first-class passengers. I looked back into the coach section and saw the majority of those passengers were also visibly shaken by the unexpected turbulence.

The pretty blonde flight attendant noticed my state of alarm and said, "How about another martini to settle your nerves?"

Giving her the thumbs up, I said, "I'm surprised the pilot didn't warn us of the turbulence beforehand. That was quite a jolt. It felt like something hit the plane."

"There's nothing to worry about. It was just an air pocket. The pilot is flying at thirty-four thousand feet, which is higher than normal, to avoid the worst of the storm."

As soon as the words were out of her mouth, I heard a loud pop and someone screamed in the coach section. The cabin pressure deflated in an audible whoosh as the oxygen masks fell from above every seat. The man next to me quickly placed the elastic strap around his head and positioned the cup on his face. I removed my portable oxygen mask and placed the dangling yellow cup to my face.

Immediately, I couldn't breathe with the emergency oxygen mask and replaced it with the one I'd been wearing. I looked helplessly at my fellow passengers and watched them gasping for breath like fish out of water. For some reason, they were not getting oxygen from the emergency cups that had been deployed. The cacophony of screams and wails resonated throughout the plane as the passengers struggled to breathe. The blonde flight attendant pounded on the door of the cockpit and then collapsed to the floor.

I looked back into the coach section and saw the passengers slumped across their seats or lying motionless on the floor in heaps. A stream of papers, pillows, and loose objects were being sucked toward a window in the back of the plane that was apparently open to the outside. An eerie mist began to fill the cabin.

I sat motionless with my eyes closed for a few minutes for fear someone would try to steal my oxygen supply. In a short time, all pleas for help ended. I reached forward and felt for a pulse on the passenger sitting in front of me. There was none. I pushed the call button over my seat, but, as I expected, no one was alive to answer it. I concluded that everyone aboard was dead except for the pilots and me. I included the pilots because the plane seemed to be flying normally despite the loss of cabin pressure.

I sat there wondering what to do. The meter on my portable oxygen unit indicated that three-quarters remained in the canister. I estimated that I had about an hour and a half left before I ran out of oxygen. I noticed that the exposed skin of all the first-class passengers had turned pale. Some of the dead bodies were twisted in their seats and staring back at me with blank open eyes.

I looked back into the coach section and saw rows of ashen faces staring forward toward first class. I guessed about 150 passengers were dead. I wondered what was going on in the cockpit. There had been no announcements. The drone of the engines gave no indication of a changing flight pattern, much less any preparation for landing.

I thought about the vast fortune that I'd probably never live to spend and started to cry. The creepy mist that I'd seen in coach began to seep around me. In a short time, the entire plane was engulfed. The corpses seated around me mercifully disappeared into the fog.

After a few more minutes passed, I stood and groped like a blind man toward the cockpit. I stumbled and fell atop a heap of bodies in the aisle. My hand broke my fall as it fell hard upon the clammy face of a corpse. It felt like my thumb had inadvertently gouged an open eye. I gasped in horror as I bolted forward on a bed of dead bodies. I finally smacked into the cockpit door and slumped beside it. I knocked and then pounded on the door repeatedly and shouted, "I am the only survivor of all the passengers. My portable oxygen supply will run out soon. Can you help me?"

I waited for a reply, but none came. Pounding on the door until my knuckles were raw, I shouted like a madman. Exhausted from the trauma, I put my ear to the door and listened to the dead silence within. Other than the drone of the engines, the entire plane was like a tomb.

If the pilots were alive, they would have answered me. I was no threat to them behind the security door. The only explanation was that the plane was on autopilot and would crash when it ran out of fuel.

Suddenly the roar from the open window in coach stopped. Something must have lodged in the window and plugged the hole, at least for now. Probably some poor bastard had become a human stopper.

Almost immediately, the fog began to dissipate as the cabin pressure began to stabilize. I saw the pallid faces of the corpses seated around me materialize from the fog with their ghastly open eyes. Turning away from the horror, I began to rifle through the cabinets in the refreshment area for a spare oxygen canister. I found some miniature liquor bottles, but no oxygen.

The engines outside continued to drone as I made my way back to a vacant seat. I screwed off the tops of three bottles of Jack Daniels and chugged them. I trembled at the thought of my oxygen running out. I sat there among the first-class corpses to wait for my impending doom. The stench of urine and shit grew heavy in the pressurized cabin. I readjusted my oxygen nosepiece to block out as much of the foul odor as I could.

I felt a vibration in my shirt pocket, and my cell phone began to ring. I grabbed it and said, "Hello. Who's this?"

"It's Harry. I was sitting here bored out of my mind reviewing loan applications and wondered how the luckiest guy on the planet is doing."

"Harry! Thank God you called. I didn't know I had any reception. Listen carefully before we're cut off. I'm on Monarch flight 1580 to San Francisco, and as far as I can tell everyone is dead except me."

"Rudy, you old prankster. That's the best one you've ever come up with. I've got to hand it to you—"

"Harry! Shut up and listen! This is no joke. A window blew out in the back of the plane, and when the oxygen masks were deployed, they didn't work, and everyone aboard but me died. My portable oxygen supply saved me."

"Who's flying the plane?"

"I believe the plane is on autopilot until it runs out of gas. Stay on the line, but go to another phone and call the FAA. Tell them I'm on medical oxygen and my supply is running out. Give them my cell number. Maybe they can tell me where they keep the spare canisters until they can intercept the plane. I'm desperate. Have you got that?"

I listened for an answer, but the line was dead. There was no service to make another call, and I didn't know how much of what I had said Harry heard.

I thought about what Harry had said about my being the luckiest person in the world and thought I might be. One hundred and fifty people were dead, and I was still alive. Time would tell if my luck would run out.

I heard a metal clank on the underbelly of the plane. A few minutes later, I heard strange sounds and muffled voices from below the coach section. There was no doubt a rescue party was outside trying to breach the underside of the plane. I remembered the way the passengers in the movie *Executive Decision* were rescued from terrorists by joining two airplanes flying at the same speed with a compression interface. Was this movie concoction really possible?

"Thank God!" I thought. "Maybe I will survive after all."

I left my seat and struggled into the coach section. A fiery outline appeared in the middle of the aisle and a section of the floor was removed, and several men catapulted into the cabin from below.

I shouted for help, and two men struggled past a heap of bodies and stared at me like they were seeing a ghost.

Looking at my portable oxygen unit, one said, "You must be the luckiest person on the planet."

* * *

A month passed and I decided to visit my sister in West Orange, New Jersey, before resuming my world tour. During that time, I cut out numerous newspaper and magazine articles that referred to me as "the luckiest man alive." Life was good. Everything was coming up roses.

My lawyer was suing Monarch Airlines for several more million in damages to add to my lottery winnings.

Finally, on September 11, 2001, my sister drove me to the Newark Airport, and I boarded flight 93 to San Francisco.

* * *

CONFESSIONAL

The young blond altar boy opened the priest's office door and ran across the church and fled into the street. He was shaken and confused by what had happened. The ramifications of telling his mother about the incident weighed heavily on his mind. One of the other altar boys had told him what happened behind closed doors in the priest's chambers, but he never believed it until now. He sat on a bench across the street and wept. A tall man sitting nearby saw how distressed the boy was and asked what he could do to help.

An hour later, the priest was working on the mass for Sunday's service when he heard the chime on the entry door. He arose from his desk and looked out to see a giant of a man dressed in a black sweat suit heading toward a confessional. He had to stoop to get inside and struggled to a kneeling position as he closed the door. The priest didn't think he'd ever seen the man before, and he was good at remembering faces.

It was six o'clock, which left only thirty minutes until dinner would be served. He hoped the stranger would be a light sinner and he would make it on time. Rosemary said they were having roast beef with mashed potatoes and gravy and apple pie. His favorite.

He entered the confessional and a green light came on above the door.

Both booths were dim inside, separated by a wall with a lattice insert for some measure of discretion between the occupants. The stranger could see the priest, but the priest could not see the stranger distinctly.

After a short pause, they both made the sign of the cross and whispered, almost in unison, "In the name of the Father, and of the Son, and of the Holy Spirit."

The priest read a passage from the Holy Scripture. When it was completed, he waited for the stranger to speak.

After a pause, the stranger began, "Bless me, Father, for I have sinned. It's been more than a year since my last confession. I have taken the name of God in vain often and have surrounded myself with others who use profanity."

The priest thought, "This won't take long at all if this was his most regrettable sin."

"I haven't been to church for so long, I don't remember."

The priest thought, "Sin number two. A common fault among churchgoers. Nothing earth shattering." He was tabulating the number of "Our Fathers" and "Hail Marys" in his mind.

"I used to smoke pot and drink scotch on the rocks excessively."

"Did this contribute to a poor performance at work?"

"Yes, Father. I was on probation for missing too many days when I had the accident."

"Accident?"

"In a drunken stupor, I back-ended a car that was stopped for a red light."

"Were there any casualties?"

"The two in the back seat were crushed to death."

"My God!" the priest blurted. "Were you hurt?"

"The airbag saved me, but I lost my license for two years."

"You are supposed to start with the serious sins first. You seem to be going in the opposite direction. Is that it?"

"I'm sorry, Father. There's more. It's really been much more than a year since my last confession, and I'm a bit rusty."

"You do feel sorry for your sins and have come to me seeking absolution?"

The stranger thought about the phrase "the pot calling the kettle black" and the hypocrisy of the monster in the next compartment passing judgment on his sins. "Absolutely. I can't live with myself any longer."

The priest sighed deeply and said, "Continue."

"I have been unfaithful to my wife."

"How did you meet this person?"

"It was a man I met at rehab."

"A man?"

"Yes, Father. I'm a homosexual."

"When did you discover this?" the priest asked as he thought of the delicious roast beef and potatoes that would be cold by the time he sat down to the dinner table.

"I was about eleven when my father made his first move on me."

"Your father?"

"Well, I think it was my real father, but it is difficult to say for sure. My mother fooled around a lot when my father was out of town. He was a truck driver."

"Why did you marry a woman if you are not heterosexual?"

The stranger paused to concoct a plausible response. "I promised my mother I'd have a child so she could be a grandmother."

The priest scratched at his temple and thought about the apple pie he was sure to miss. This man was a serious sinner and desperately needed help if he really did seek salvation.

"Have you been to counseling?"

"Many times."

"When was this?"

"It was when I was serving time in Rahway."

The priest thought he heard a chuckle from the man in the booth, which seemed bizarre considering the nature of his confession. The interior of the church had become dark, and he suddenly remembered he hadn't switched on the lights at the appropriate time due to the stranger's sudden appearance.

Excusing himself, the priest opened the door of the confessional and peered out into the church. The only lights were the votive candles flickering in the distance and those of the confessional.

He saw the full moon shining through the skylight in the ceiling high above the altar. He raced across the aisle and snapped on the lights. Instantly, four statues of Jesus and Mary were illuminated on both sides of the altar and at the corners of the church near the entrance. The stained-glass windows were ablaze with beautiful and awe-inspiring tapestries of heavenly landscapes. He smiled and returned to the confessional.

"I apologize for the interruption. I forgot to turn on the lights when the sun went down, as I was so enthralled by your confession. You say you were in prison?"

"I was just getting to that part."

"What were you in for?"

"Child pornography."

The priest groaned under his breath at this reply and tried to think of something constructive to say, but the stranger responded first. "My life has been a hell on earth. I can't help it if I get an erection when I see a man's hairy ass. Do you think I want to be like this? It's not my fault; I was born this way."

"Was that another chuckle?" the priest thought. He knew the confession was bullshit. He could spot a pedophile or a gay guy a mile away. After all, he was one. He didn't know what the man was up to, but he was getting hungrier by the minute. Nonetheless, he decided to play along. "Do you blame God for your homosexuality?"

"Not anymore than I do for my bloodlust."

"Bloodlust?"

"Yes, Father. I have the overpowering desire to devour human beings when the moon is full. God is totally responsible for my condition. He made me a werewolf. It wasn't my choice."

"Why did you come to my door? I am a man of God."

"When I was an altar boy, a monster like you called me into his chambers. I never forgot how I was violated, but didn't have the courage to come forward. God answered my prayers for revenge when he let me live after being bitten by a werewolf. Now that I've become one myself, every full moon I quench my insatiable hunger for blood and revenge with a pedophile. I was waiting for the moon to rise when I saw the troubled young boy run from your church. God works in mysterious ways, and I'm his devoted servant, not you."

The priest's started to recite a litany of "Our Fathers" and "Hail Marys" as the faces of many young victims flooded his memory.

The stranger chuckled. "I was having so much fun with my false confession I committed another sin when I disobeyed what my mother taught me. She told me never to play with my food." His voice morphed into a bloodcurdling howl that filled the church.

The priest squirmed in his chair and tried desperately to catch his breath. His teeth began to chatter as he saw the hungry eyes of the beast ogling him through the latticework. And then the hairy shape rose from its kneeling position, and he heard a snuffling sound like a bloodhound smelling the scent of prey. The stench of spoiled meat assaulted his nostrils as he shrank backward into the shadows and waited for the retribution he knew would come.

9503952R0

Made in the USA
Lexington, KY
04 May 2011